I0451492

HIGHWAYS END

By

Dagan J. Sharpe

Highways End

Copyright © 2017 Dagan J Sharpe

All rights reserved.

ISBN: 0692944761
ISBN-13: 978-0692944769

Preface by Author

Highways End was started when I was engaged to the woman destined to be my wife. It was a celebration story of how I found peace in her love. However, as time passed and my faith grew, I realized although love is indeed a blessing, a restless heart can't even find rest there.

This transformed the story to one with deeper meaning. For it wasn't until I surrendered my life to Jesus Christ that I discovered the Creator of love and how only through Him can true peace be found and sacrificial love between others can be realized.

This book evolved to be an illustrative tale of Ecclesiastes. The famed book of the Bible written by King Solomon. Like the book reminds us, searching for meaning on earth, "under the sun", is always a vain attempt, no matter the prizes that may be won. For a life lived apart from our Creator is truly a chasing after the wind.

In fact, there are deeper treasures to be discovered beyond our salvation. For salvation is a glorious gift given to believers, but the rewards of sanctification involves sacrifices on our part. Sacrifices of our will, our desires and our dreams for His. He grants us dreams and visions, but only when they come from Him, or surrendered to Him, do they bring joy, fulfillment and purpose. Thus, pursing love is a worthy cause, but to pursue it without Christ limits its full potential and ours.

Highways End is a reflection of lives filled with empty pursuits and dreams, and coming to realize apart from God all is vanity. My hope is this story speaks to other restless souls and hearts and serves as an encouragement to put Christ first in all things and trust Him with all outcomes.

Dagan J. Sharpe

HIGHWAYS END

Chapter I

Valen knelt by the large, crooked pine tree on their farm where Rhiannon was buried. The breeze blew gently, and the freshness of spring filled the air. The sun shone bright and there wasn't a cloud to be seen. However, Valen's loneliness was deep and tears filled his eyes. Minutes passed like hours, but the longer he sat, the clearer his thinking became. His heart pounded wildly and suddenly. His mind returned to the little boy playing in the yard back at the house. Rising to his feet, Valen looked toward the sky. He knew what he had to do. His purpose was clear.

Rushing home, Valen picked his boy up and held him tight against his chest. "I'll never quit on you, Destin...I promise," he cried, as tears rolled down his face.

"I love you." I just hung in his arms, silent, too confused to say a word.

"For the remainder of his life, my dad remained true to his promise as I grew to realize he was always there for me," Destin reflected. "He loved unconditionally and without expectation. What he taught was simple - Obey God, trust in His promises and serve others in love.

However, over the years, I somehow forgot these basic rules and instead I was losing the woman I loved and caught up in a chasing after the wind. Sadly, most of these problems arose due to my selfish ambitions. Building respect and prominence had become my biggest priorities, and my entire being seemed devoted to them. The strange thing was, I knew it was strangling me, my marriage, and my soul - but like an addict, I couldn't stop.

My wife, Lynn, managed the lonely nights by re-living her past through old photographs she kept piled away in a trunk by our bed. We barely talked now, but there was a time when things were different. When we were best friends and God was first in our life. We loved to talk about our dreams, how many children we wanted, the places we wanted to see and the adventures we wanted to experience. I was at peace then, and so was she. We were happy being together and nothing else mattered, but there was a blind deception in our life and it would soon work to try and destroy us both.

It has always amazed me how one person has the power to affect another so deeply - either for the positive, or negative. For us, our joy soon turned to weariness and misery. I can't recall the exact moment I began losing my way, but looking back, I clearly know how it slowly evolved with one compromise after another. My foundation began to fade and so my purpose became re-directed, and success became my goal. I fooled myself into thinking I was building a future, but that of course wasn't true. I was lost in my performance at work and with acquiring more, and losing her didn't seem to matter as much. So, I continued to indulge myself in my ambitions even more as we drifted further apart.

I remember times of wanting to bring her close to me and kissing her like I used to, but my pride prevented it. I couldn't seem to find that part of me anymore. I was lost, and the man my wife married was slowly disappearing. I had forgotten my prayer to keep my eyes off worthless things, and as a result, I was forgetting who I was - that's when I hit my rock bottom.

It had been a long day, and I decided to meet some friends from work at the local Mexican restaurant, and unlike my typical show of restraint, this time, I decided to go for those extra beers. Then, not only did I foolishly attempt to drive home, but upon arriving, I reached for Lynn for the first time in a long time. Obviously, she didn't take to any of my advances, and instead, pushed me back outside and locked the doors. I slept in the yard that night to the surprise of our neighbor's dog who I apparently decided to snuggle with late in the night. I was literally in the dog house.

For many, this may not seem much like hitting bottom, but for me, it was. I saw the disgust in my wife's eyes and the complete loss of respect she had for me. I knew our marriage was on the fringe of being over, and I knew I was walking a bleak path. There was no joy, no laughter and no intimacy - only greed, sorrow, loneliness and despair.

So, that's what leads me here. I have some confessions to make and some things to remember. Some of these things are parts of me I have tried to ignore, like the love and truth my father taught me so long ago. Ironically, despite my position, I don't think I ever truly appreciated, or accepted these truths until I faced the hardships having them absent can cause. I need to feel peace and purpose again, and I know this is how my father would have wanted me to start that process."

Chapter II

Ironically, for a good part of his life, my father was consumed with the same hunger for success I had. He was orphaned by the age of five and raised in poverty by his older brother, Jake. So, he sought the respect and validation he felt money could bring. Their dad had died of cancer not long after Jake's tenth birthday, and their mother, who was accustomed to nervous breakdowns, left one day without notice to live with a man she had just met. So, the two boys had to do the best they could and hope that no one ever noticed they were without parents.

Jake quit school and started working construction, as well as odd jobs to keep food on the table and bills paid. My father, Valen, was made to stay in school and was accountable for keeping the house clean. The partnership worked well, but the stress and responsibilities soon took their toll on Jake and to escape his painful reality, he began drinking heavily.

As years past, my father grew handsome and strong. He stood right at six-feet tall, had dark hair and hazel eyes. In fact, his looks were contradictory to his personality. To see him, one would assume confidence, but instead, he was a sensitive and shy man, who preferred being alone. He spent most of his time fishing, writing and taking photographs. In fact, his only true friend was a poor colored man named Sherman.

Sherman was a retired Army Sergeant who lived out in a small house near the river. Although modest, his home was always immaculate and was set along the banks of some of the most beautiful land ever seen. Oaks, weeping willows and dogwoods surrounded his property. It was the kind of place one felt safe and away from the rest of the world.

My father first met Sherman one evening while fishing. Sherman simply hobbled over on his cane, gnawing an unlit cigar, and asked if he could join in. My father was initially frightened by his appearance, but soon grew to love his gentle nature and admire his wisdom.

Sherman was an intimidating looking man with deep wrinkles and hard features. The whites of his eyes were stained yellow and cataracts painted the outline of his pupils pearl white. His beard was neatly trimmed, but his wardrobe consisted of well-worn overalls, t-shirts and paint-stained work boots. Most people in town knew Sherman as a good-spirited and Godly man, but questioned his sanity. For everyone also knew of the horrors he had faced years earlier, and so, many just left him alone, not certain of his mental stability. In reality though, Sherman was quite sane, more so than most, and he had learned the joys of living simply and sharing laughs. His past was rarely mentioned, or discussed.

Sherman was raised in a small town in Georgia and was once married and the father of two beautiful girls. His family meant everything to him, and he was a loving husband and father. However, when World War II broke out, he was called to duty. It was during this time, when he was away, his nightmare began.

One night, two local boys, with nothing better to do, were out drinking and smoking near the river when they heard the laughter of girls. Moving in to get a better look, they noticed Sherman's wife cradling her two little girls with a bedtime story. The bedroom windows were left open to enjoy the evening's cool breeze. Being drunk and filled with ignorant prejudice, this vulnerable sight stirred up the boys' already tempered nature. This is when they decided to make their move. In an instant, they broke down the door and grabbed Sherman's wife, Nicole, pinning her to the bedside table. The girls screamed and watched helplessly as their mother fought violently to free herself, yelling for her daughters to run. Enraged, the men tore her flesh as they struggled to rip her clothes off.

They soon turned their attention to the two girls, Sarah and Josse who were frozen with fear holding each other tightly in a far corner of the room. The men took turns on both them, leaving them broken and left for dead. This horror occurred only hours before their father's expectant return.

Sherman, who had been awarded many medals for his bravery and valor, anxiously anticipated his homecoming, unaware of the nightmare awaiting him. Upon his arrival early the next morning, Sherman ran from the cab, and called for his girls, bearing gifts.

However, as soon as he burst through the door, he sensed something was wrong. No one was there to greet him and there was a silence in the home that sent shivers down his spine. Calling for his wife, Sherman, ran down the hall to his daughters' bedroom, where he discovered the unimaginable. His family lay dead and their life of innocence shattered by a darkness only hell could imagine.

The shock was overwhelming, and despite the death Sherman had witnessed during the war, nothing could have prepared his mind, or soul for what he found. He literally lost all control. For years he tried to track down the two men who committed the act, and for years he tried to get the police's help, but nothing ever happened. Justice was never awarded and this is when Sherman seemingly withdrew. He abandoned his home, took to a small cottage just outside of town and was rarely seen again.

My father, Valen, met Sherman years after this horrific event, and apparently after much healing had taken place in Sherman's life, for most of their time was spent peacefully fishing. My father, being from the lower end of town and from a questionable home environment wasn't accepted very well among his peers. So, having nothing better to do, Valen would meet Sherman by the river several times a week, and they would spend hours talking about all kinds of things ranging from music, food and the mysteries of life.

There were also hours spent in pure silence where they simply enjoyed the outdoors and each other's friendship. They shared a mutual respect for one another and it was during one of these quiet times when Sherman revealed to my dad his tragic story and how he learned to deal with the situation, but more importantly, how he learned what his purpose in life was and the answer to his question why.

Chapter III

Although, much of the local community seemed to think Sherman had all but vanished from civil society, the truth was far from it. In his later years, Sherman had begun an outreach to troubled youth, similar to the boys who had taken his family. His initial desire for revenge had turned to forgiveness and since he was never able to find those guilty of the crime, he turned his focus to help others from going down a similar path. He also began working with those from abusive homes in an attempt to offer healing and hope. His walk turned from one of despair, anger and loss to peace, clarity and purpose.

Valen had found this way of living both inspiring and confusing, but the authenticity compelling. He began joining Sherman on his visits to those in need and listened to the wisdom he shared. The truth could not be ignored, and the testimony of his life was most appealing. Not only was Sherman's life changed, but others were also being impacted by his story and love. There was life being restored. Life was being given and new life was being discovered.

Simply put, Sherman was sharing the good news of the gospel, but it wasn't as if he were selling soap, or pitching product. It was a sharing from his heart, and others listened, because Sherman testified to what had happened to him and how he was affected. Others saw he was genuine. There was nothing fake, or forced about him and others received the truth and were transformed, and their transformation then affected others and so on.

Valen was one of these affected. He learned that life was more than trying to make a life, but more about discovering the life already established for us. He was introduced to the Bible for the first time and began learning how to trust and apply its encouraging lessons from the lives of others who had faced hardships, were misunderstood and treated unfairly. He learned of the peace that transcends all understanding, and how despite the pain, believing in Jesus and trusting in His promises was the anchor necessary to walk honorably and authentically. He learned that life was not so much about his desires, but about promoting the reputation of Christ through living a life of obedience and leaving all the consequences to Him.

This was also when my father accepted Jesus in his life and was baptized by Sherman in the very river they spent so many hours enjoying. In time, this new life would be tested and proven pure. Through his hardships his faith would be strengthened and through his loss, his true devotion was established.

Sherman shared how after the loss of his family, his rage nearly destroyed him. He couldn't concentrate on anything other than revenge and the despair of his loss. Although tragic, the event was continually relived and nurtured through his pain. He turned to alcohol to drown the memory, but it only made the sting worse. He considered taking his own life on several occasions, but could never go through with it. He was sinking in despair until one day while on his face, crying out for answers, he was distracted by a child's laughter. Just outside his window he could hear it - it sounded just like his little Josse, but he knew it couldn't be. He thought he might be dreaming and stood silent, listening for the voice again.

This time he heard it farther in the distance. So, he ran outside to try and find it. He found a family sharing a picnic near the river bank. The father was blind folded and playing chase with his

16

daughter, while pretending to bump into trees. The wife was unfolding the sandwiches and getting all prepared to begin eating, when she saw Sherman standing amongst the trees. Startled she called to her husband.

The man walked over to Sherman to introduce himself and his daughter and invited him to join them for lunch. Sherman of course declined and apologized for the interruption, but the family insisted. It was during this time, Sherman saw the beauty in life again. He saw love, he saw innocence and he saw the darkness of his own heart amidst the beauty before him.

The family said a prayer before their meal and Sherman remembered what he had once had. He felt the joy momentarily, but it was soon replaced with the sorrow of his loss.

The man reached out to take Sherman's hand and prayed. "Father, we thank you for our new friend and for bringing us together. I don't know what pain this child of yours has faced, but you do, and we pray for your healing to be upon him. I pray that you open his heart to your truth and restore the peace, only you can bring. I pray you show him his purpose and help him find the courage he needs through your son, Jesus Christ. May he come to know You, serve You and give his life to You so that his life on earth may be restored. In Jesus name, Amen."

Sherman's eyes were filled with tears and his life began to change that very day. He thanked the family for their kindness and ran back to his home, where he began tearing down books to find the Bible he knew was buried there somewhere.

From that day forward, practically, every moment of Sherman's life was spent studying Scripture, seeking the answers to the questions his life of despair and anger never provided. He called out to God. He prayed. He screamed in anger. He cried in pain and he prayed for help. He begged for restoration, and he eventually surrendered his life to Christ.

In time, he too began sharing this healing truth with others in need, and in time, he found a peace he had never known. He now knew that in a fallen world apart of from God, there was only wrath and sin, but under God's grace, there was protection and that He would work all things for good to those called to His purpose. Therefore, Sherman was determined to allow God to work good in his life and transform the tragedy in his life into a blessing for others.

Thus, he began his mission to help others overcome their sorrow, their tragedy and their pain. He refused to let his pain be a waste and his family's life a forgotten memory. He also realized that he would be blessed as he blessed others and that in time, he would be reunited with the family he loved and missed so dearly.

Sherman served as a mentor and a source of inspiration for my father, and he routinely shared his struggles, doubts and concerns with Sherman to gain his unique insight and wisdom. One of their major topics of conversations was consistently centered around a particular girl my father went to school with named Rhiannon.

In fact, my father and mother were friends at an early age. The age before the color of one's skin and the amount of money someone has are even recognized - the age of innocence. They first met while attending elementary school, but as time moved on, popularity became an issue, and old habits had to be cast aside, which included Valen. This rejection was difficult for him, even though he tried to act as if he didn't care, for his love for

Rhiannon had already been born.

However, high school found very different roles for Valen and Rhiannon. Valen never quite fit in with the crowd and remained to himself. Rhiannon on the other-hand soared and soon became both class president and homecoming queen. She loved school and being involved. Valen hated it. Although, they knew each other and continued to have feelings for one another, their relationship eventually dwindled from a nod in the halls to not even a glance.

Unlike Valen, Rhiannon's popularity was fueled by the fact that her father, Cane Waters, was one of the wealthiest men in town. He was a real estate developer and practically built many of the outdoor shopping centers in Georgia. Valen had always been impressed with his down-to-earth composure and was inspired by his wealth. Rhiannon's entire family was first class. The only blemish was her parents' divorce.

They separated due to Cane's over-commitment to work. He loved his wife dearly, but he couldn't seem to break away to spend time with her. She eventually got lonely enough, and despite her love for him, filed for divorce.

Rhiannon was very close to both of her parents and the separation was hard for her to accept. Although her father only moved a short distance from their home, the transfer from one house to the other was exhausting. Eventually, Rhiannon's mother, Elizabeth, remarried, but her father never did. He remained in love with Elizabeth until a stroke took his life two years after the divorce.

Elizabeth's new husband, Pete White, was nothing like Rhiannon's father. Pete was a devilishly charming man, with the backbone of a snake. He provided Elizabeth with the attention she needed, but it was without an ounce of sincerity. He was in it for the money, and he played his role to the hilt. He was the kind of guy that could fool anyone with his boyish looks and friendly smile, but behind the facade was a greedy, perverted and insecure man.

Since her parents' divorce, Rhiannon was seldom at home. Not only did Pete give her the creeps, but the whole house just seemed to hang with depression. So, Rhiannon spent most of her time at school, or out late with friends.

One of those late evenings, Valen was distracted from his writing with the sounds of laughter and loud music coming from the woods behind his house. Curious to see who was out that far from town, Valen meandered to where the noise was coming from. He found some kids from his high school throwing a party. My father didn't know any of them well, primarily because of his lack of attendance. However, he did recognize one of the girls - Rhiannon. She remained the most beautiful woman he had ever seen. He knew her in every detail, from the highlights in her long auburn hair to the sparkle in her dark brown eyes. He even knew the one tiny freckle that was on the back of her right knee. Rhiannon was naturally tan with an athletic build, while at the same time soft. Valen felt that she was truly one of God's finest creations.

Noticing many of the guys had on a tux, Valen soon realized it was prom night. He laughed sadly at how he didn't even care to attend his own prom. Valen continued to watch the party from behind a tree. He smiled as he saw Rhiannon dance, wishing he could be with her, but in small towns, at that time, the line between rich and poor just wasn't crossed. So, instead of making a scene, he kept quiet.

Everyone was there. Jed Stenson, the town's second wealthiest kid, was just crowned prom king that night and all of his grand ego was on display. His shirt was off and beer was being poured over his head in celebration. Rhiannon, of course was crowned prom queen, and so, Jed was all over her, hoping to get lucky.

Valen sat quietly behind the tree and was about to get up to leave when he noticed Rhiannon wandering deep into the woods. She was attempting to use the bathroom, but Jed was closely following, unnoticed.

"Oh! What do we have here?" Jed coyly remarked as he found Rhiannon pulling up her jeans.

"Jed? What are you doing here? Can't you see I'm in the middle of something!"

"Ah, com'on Rhian, it's not like I've never seen it before", as he reached to pull her near.

Valen stood and watched intently, angered by Jed's arrogance.

"Jed, I mean it. Leave me alone!"

"SHHHH! You want someone to hear?"

"Yes! Now, leave me alone", Rhiannon yelled as she tried to pry Jed's hands off of her.

"I said shut up and come here!" Jed forced his hand over Rhiannon's mouth. Gasping for air, Rhiannon fought to get free.

Valen, insane with rage, busted out of the brush and grabbed Jed by the hair. "She told you to leave her alone!" He demanded as he threw him to the ground.

Stunned, Jed stumbled to his feet. "What the...You? Just who do you think you are?"

"She told you leave her alone. Now, leave!"

Still taken off guard by Valen's abruptness, Jed proudly brushed himself off.

"Wait a minute. What were you doing out in the woods here? Are you spying on Rhiannon? Takin' a little peak? Ha! Rhiannon, I think your hero here is actually a peeping-tom."

Valen stood speechless.

Rhiannon, trying to get some clarity on the situation, turned to them both.

"Just leave - both of you. Leave!" She cried.

As Valen and Jed turned, Jed grabbed Valen's shoulder and pushed him against a tree.

"I'm not done with you!"

Blood streamed from Valen's nose where he hit the tree, and he knew he had to do something fast, before Jed's friends heard all the noise.

Valen plowed himself into Jed's chest, and the two of them began rolling on the ground exchanging punches. Valen was driven to a point he had never been and tears of anger were rolling down his face. Insane with rage he began slamming Jed's head against the ground, pounding harder and harder until he stopped moving completely. Jed was knocked unconscious. Realizing what he had just done, Valen stood and stared at the body between his legs. His hands were covered in blood. Rhiannon was behind him and had seen the whole thing.

"Valen, what did you do? Are you crazy?"

"I don't know. He was trying to hurt you, and I just couldn't let that happen. I'm sorry."

Rhiannon was silent and saw the honesty in his eyes.

"You have to leave," she pleaded. "Please, before anyone comes...Go!"

Valen wandered back to the woods, and as his silhouette disappeared, Rhiannon whispered a soft, thank you.

Sherman saw Valen late the next day.

"What happened to you? Are you okay?"

"Yea, I'm fine, but I think I hurt someone pretty bad last night."

"Who? What happened?"

"Ah, a kid from school...Jed Stenson."

"Stenson! Isn't his dad an attorney here? What'd you do?"

"He was trying to hurt, Rhiannon, Sherman. I couldn't just stand there and watch it happen. He was drunk. So, I stepped in to break it up, and that's when I lost it. I don't know how bad he's hurt."

"Valen, that boy's dad can give you some real trouble!"

As if just realizing the severity of his situation, Valen shook his head in disbelief.

"How's Rhiannon?" Sherman continued.

"She's fine, but I'm telling you he was up to no good."

"Well, we gotta' find out what happened to this guy." Sherman warned.

"Yea, I know." Valen replied somberly.

"Do we need to get you outta' here?"

"No, I'll take care of this. I didn't do anything wrong."

"Maybe so, but no one else knows that."

"No, Rhiannon knows. She'll help me out. I'll call her tonight to find out what happened after I left."

Valen returned home about eight that afternoon, and found his brother sitting on the couch surrounded by empty bottles and overflowing ashtrays.

"Where you been?"

"Out."

"You been fishin' with that crazy black man again, ain't ya'. You betta' stay away from him. Some might think that crazy will stick on you too," he snickered.

"That right? Well, I really don't care much about what others

24

think."

Valen hated when Jake drank, or smoked. He honestly became another person. However, his habits were getting worse, and Jake was drunk almost every day now. He and Valen loved each other deeply, and although Jake wanted Valen to have a better life, sometimes his jealousy got in the way.

Valen swayed to his room and lay back on his bed to ponder the last 24 hours. Although, he may have nearly killed a man, all he could think about was Rhiannon. He needed to call her. With jittery hands, Valen picked up the phone. The palms of his hands were wet with sweat. What would he say? How would he say it, and what would she say? Suddenly, she answered – "Hello?"

"Rhiannon?"

"Yes?"

"This is Valen." All he could think about were her next few words. Would she be glad it was him?

"Hi, Valen. How are you?"

"I'm okay. How are you?"

"I'm fine. And by the way, thank you."

"There's no need to thank me. I couldn't let anything happen to you."

"I know, and again, thank you. Oh, and in case your curious, other than a hurt ego, Jed's okay."

"Well, I guess that's good," Valen snickered in huge relief.

"Yeah," Rhiannon laughed. "I guess so."

Now was the moment, Valen thought, to ask her to meet him again. It was now or never.

"Uhmm. Rhiannon?"

"Yes, Valen."

"I was wondering..."

"Yes." she whispered.

"It's been a very long time, but I was wondering if you would like to join me tomorrow for dinner?"

"I'd love to Valen."

"Great! How does five o'clock sound?"

"Perfect."

"Great. I'll pick you up at five then."

"Valen?"

"Yes?"

"Thanks, again."

"You're welcome."

Valen slammed the phone down and ran out to the living room, expecting, for a moment, to tell someone the good news, but of course, there was no one there but Jake, passed out on the couch. So, Valen turned outside jumped on his junk motorcycle and raced to find Sherman. Thoughts of being with Rhiannon again filled his mind, and a smile spread across his face.

"Sherm! You awake?"

"Valen? It's awful late', boy...You okay?"

"I'm great! And I'm sorry to wake you, but I thought you'd like to know that Jed is fine. I just spoke with Rhiannon."

Sherman walked out pulling up his overall strap. "Oh, Valen, that's great news!"

"Oh, and I have a date with her."

"What!" Sherman smiled. "That's great!" He said, patting Valen's back. "Be sure to bring her by, if you get a chance."

"Absolutely. Go back to bed, and thanks for listening. I just had to tell someone."

The next day, Valen raced around preparing everything to be just right. At first, he was embarrassed of his only means of transportation - an old worn out Honda motorcycle, but he sucked up his pride, kicked his motor to a start, and sped towards Rhiannon's house.

Valen stopped at the gate that guarded her home and dialed the number displayed on the screen.

"Yes?" the voice over the speaker asked.

"I'm here to see Rhiannon."

"Your name, sir?"

"Valen."

"One moment please."

As Valen was put on hold, he looked around the surroundings. It was as if he was in some other world. There was no dirt in sight, only the most luscious green grass he had ever seen. Even the pine trees seemed perfectly trimmed and shaped in every detail.

This is what he wanted. He ached for it. With money, he would finally get some respect. If only he knew how to make his. He was talented with his writing and photography. All his life, he felt as though he had something special, something different. That he was meant to make a difference and amount to something. So, when he saw all these glorious riches, he thought that represented success, which only fed his misplaced hunger. The surroundings inspired him and sent his imagination racing with all that could be. Even though he knew he was to be content with what God had given him, he couldn't help but want for more. He never had much, and he desperately wanted to be the one who had.

"Sir," stated the speaker, interrupting his thoughts, "you may enter."

"Thank you."

Valen kicked his bike to a start and made his way up the driveway. To call what he saw a house, would be a great injustice. The old Georgia mansion was delicious to the eyes. Twenty white columns surrounded the red brick estate. Glorious dogwoods and oaks decorated the lawn, and Spanish moss dangled freely in the breeze. In the center of the drive a fountain sprung and was filled with live, brightly colored fish.

To see Valen's bike beside all this glory was truly a mockery. The old bike's fuel line was held together with duct tape, and the muffler held in place with a rusted coat hanger. Most of the time, the old bike would spit and putt its way to a rattling roar and would vibrate vigorously if driven over 50 miles per hour. However, he loved that bike. It was the first thing he ever bought, and he wouldn't trade it for the world.

Rhiannon, hearing his arrival, ran outside to greet him. "Valen! Good to see you, again."

Valen felt his heart drop and palms once again begin to sweat. She was truly beautiful. Her hair was draped across her tan shoulders, and her smile lit up the dimming sky. Valen felt an eternity pass before he could talk. "Hey, Rhiannon. You look great."

"Why thank you. You look great as always too."

Valen, not used to compliments, looked down modestly.

"Com'on in. Do you remember my Mom," Rhiannon said excitedly.

Rhiannon took his hand as they walked through the two, huge oak doors. "My dad designed this home. It was his dream home."

"It's breathtaking," Valen smiled.

In the hallway, two winding staircases led to the second floor. Rhiannon's mother was making her way down on the right side.

"Well, Valen, you certainly have grown. Last time we saw each

29

other you were just a little boy. We've heard a lot of things about you lately," she said reaching for his hand.

Valen had only met her once before and it was so long ago, he could barely remember.

Valen wiped his palm before extending his hand.

"It's nice to see you again, Mrs. Waters."

It was easy to see where Rhiannon got her looks. Elizabeth was in her early fifties and was unbelievably beautiful. She had an olive complexion and big dark brown eyes. However, unlike Rhiannon, she didn't appear to be as free spirited. Her long graying black hair was rolled tightly in a bun, and she carried herself with controlled southern etiquette.

In the background, Valen could hear Pete, Rhiannon's stepfather, laughing. It was his routine poker night with the boys. They would drink and smoke and top each other's lies. Pete was a terrible poker player. He always lost. That's mostly why the guys came over. They would make a small fortune off him, and he would always loose so gracefully. After all, it wasn't his money he was betting.

Suddenly Rhiannon's half-brother, Christopher ran up and went straight for Valen's legs.

Christopher must have been about four and was full of energy.

Rhiannon laughed. "Chris, get off Valen's knees."

Elizabeth looked at Valen apologetically. "I'm sorry, but for some reason he loves hanging all over people," she said smiling and pulling Chris off.

Chris was a cute little boy. His eyes were large and deep blue. He had shaggy brown hair and lots of freckles.

"Hi, Chris...My name's Valen. How old are you?"

Shy with introductions, Chris ran off up the stairs. Rhiannon smiled, and everyone laughed a little more relaxed.

"So, where are you two little rebels going tonight?" Elizabeth said jokingly.

"Well," Valen paused in thought, "I wanted it to be a surprise, but I promise to have her home by curfew."

"How's ten o'clock sound?" Elizabeth stated.

Both Valen and Rhiannon shared a quick glance of confirmation. "Great! I'll be sure to be on time," Valen smiled.

"I know you will. Now, you two go have fun."

"It was nice seeing you again, Mrs. Waters."

"Nice to see you too, Valen."

Elizabeth watched as they rode away on his motorcycle and smiled. Valen reminded her of a younger time, a more innocent time and of a love she once knew with her late husband. Valen had a soft ruggedness about him, yet she could tell at once that he was a sincere man, a man that knew pain, but a strong man - a man that faced his fear. A man of honor was something she missed very deeply, and she felt good for her daughter.

Chapter IV

Cruising down the road, Rhiannon could smell the sweet fragrance of Valen's hair as it whipped through the wind. This was the first time Rhiannon had ever ridden on a motorcycle, and she loved it. She loved being close to Valen and how he made her feel safe and free.

Rhiannon, was an ambitious person, and very independent. However, all the responsibilities she took on, often left her feeling tied down. Rhiannon was a straight-A student and was active in almost every club in school. Her lifelong ambition was to be a lawyer. However, she didn't want to limit herself to just the states. She wanted to practice international law, specializing in tax. She was already fluent in three languages. Counting English, she also knew Italian and Japanese. She truly had it all, sincerity, good looks and brains.

Valen finally stopped at the end of an old dirt road. He took Rhiannon's hand and led her to a small clearing in the woods. They followed what looked to be, at one point a trail, but now it was mostly overgrown with underbrush. They walked without a word for about a mile, ducking under hanging tree limbs and sliding past thorny bushes. Rhiannon was about to ask where he was taking her, when all of a sudden, the most beautiful landscape she had ever seen was revealed.

"This is one of my favorite places" Valen smiled.

Rhiannon spanned a horizon she never knew existed. They were standing on a cliff, about 100 feet above water, and the sun's descent was bathing everything in its bright orange glow; and the span of the lake seemed to stretch out forever.

"Valen...I never knew this place existed. How did you find it?"

"I think it found me." He winked.

"It's beautiful, everything is so beautiful."

Valen glanced at Rhiannon and smiled, then looked back towards the sun. "Yes, it is."

After the sunset, Valen lit the wood he had already set-up for a fire. They then laid back to gaze at the purple sky. The slow crackle of the fire sang to them. They could feel their own heart beats pound heavy in their chest.

"You know, the Indians, used to explain the stars by saying a blanket covered the earth at night, and that the stars were little rips in the blanket that let the light shine through."

"Really? So, what'd they say the moon was?"

"I don't know. A huge hole?"

They laughed and talked all night, but even better, they were silent, and comfortable in it.

"So, Valen, what would you like to do when you grow up?" Rhiannon smiled.

"That's a good question. I know the typical routine. First, you go to college and then you get a job, but to tell you the truth, I'm not real sure that's for me. It seems so boring. I want to live, taste all life has to offer and then write about it."

"So, why not be a writer?"

"I don't think I write that way. I mean, most of the time I'm just writing for me. I don't think other people would enjoy what I have to say."

"Well, you'll never know 'til ya' try."

"I know. I know." Valen looked over and met Rhiannon's eyes. He had never felt such a rush of emotions. He was in love.

Rhiannon felt it too. He made her feel safe and secure. He was the man she had dreamed of, and the man her mom had prayed for.

"I've missed you, Valen. And I'm sorry." Valen understood immediately she was referencing their childhood friendship and how she allowed it to be severed by childhood peer pressures of popularity.

"I missed you too, and I have someone dying to meet you. He's a dear friend, and I've told him all about you."

"Then I can't wait to meet him - Let's go tomorrow."

"You got it." Valen looked at his watch. "Well, I hate it, but it's getting close to have you home."

Rhiannon sighed.

Valen reached the house at ten 'til, but they stood on the front steps for what seemed an eternity.

"I had a great time, Valen. Thanks."

"Me too." Valen felt his stomach tremble, as he stepped toward her slowly. Gently, he took her hand. "Good night, Rhiannon..."

"Good night. See you tomorrow - around 1 o'clock?"

Valen turned, hopped on his bike and rode down the drive. "I'll be here," he smiled.

Valen raced in the night's wind. He couldn't go fast enough. The moment was too perfect. He'd never felt this good in his life. It was wonderful to be happy. So, instead of going home, Valen decided to share his news with Sherman. He had to talk about this night.

Valen pulled next to the little hand-made bridge that crossed over to Sherman's home.

"Sherman!" Valen yelled. "Where are you old man? I got somethin' to tell ya'."

Valen knelt over the glowing coals left from an earlier fire Sherman had made to warm his hands made cold from the ride over. "Sherman!" he shouted once more. Straining to see in the dark, Valen noticed the outline of a man lying by the creek.

Chapter V

Sherman had extremely bad knees from his days in the military, and could barely stand at times. My dad used to kid him and call him an old man for it. None-the-less, Sherman never went anywhere without his cane. So, when Valen saw him lying by the creek and his cane left next to the fire, he naturally began to worry.

"Sherman!" He cried.

"Val..., Valen."

Valen tilted his head to confirm what he thought he heard.

"Valen" the voice whispered again.

"Sherman? Is that you?" Valen turned toward the old oak tree near the river. Sherman was lying half conscious. "Sherman! What's wrong?"

"I'm okay," he coughed, " but I think I need a doctor."

Sherman was covered with blood and his face was swollen.

"Right. Just hang on Sherman, hang on."

Valen ran to his bike and drove it next to him. Quickly, he untied the rope he used to hold his books in place for school. "Can you stand?"

"I don't think so. I can't even feel my arm."

Valen lifted the 200 plus pound man like he was a feather and set him on the back of the motorcycle. He wrapped the rope around Sherman and then tied the other end around his own waste. "Hold on, Sherm. You're going to be fine," he said as he sped off to the hospital thirty minutes outside of town.

Valen pulled up to the emergency room and raced to untie Sherman from his waste. "Help! Someone help me!" He cried.

Some staff came out, but suddenly stopped in disgust when they saw nothing but a dirty old bum. "Come on! Help me! He's dying! What's wrong with you. Help me!"

"I'm sorry," one of the staffers said, "but we're closing."

"What?"

"No, really," the other staffer said. "We're a small facility and don't have any doctors currently on staff."

"So, what? You're going to let him die?" But it was too late. Sherman had stopped breathing. "Sherman! Sherman! No!" Valen buried his head in the old man's chest. The tears wouldn't stop. All he could do was cry. How could this happen? And why?

Some other attendees came outside to see what all the commotion was. When they saw the old man, they pushed the two staffers aside and ran to his aid. One of the attendants felt for a pulse and shook his head. "I'm sorry son."

"Where were you guys earlier?" Valen cried, as he held Sherman.

"Look son," one of the workers tried to explain, "you have to understand. There's not much we could do. We were all on our way out when we heard the noise. He's gone now. I'm sorry."

"I don't want to hear it." Valen retied the knot around Sherman and raced back towards the river.

Sherman was more than a friend. He was also the father Valen never had. He had taught him what it meant to be a man - to stand up for what he believed in, and to always bring honor to everything he did and to his name. You see, Sherman never had much, and so he believed a person's name was the only thing one truly owned. Therefore, it was important to make it something to be proud of.

Sherman didn't live a life other's might see as a success, but he worked hard, loved and lived honestly. And although a peaceful man, Sherman spent most of his life fighting wars. Whether it was WWII, or racial wars, Sherman was always fighting. Some may say these wars and the loss of his family made him crazy, but they didn't, they led him to Christ. They taught him that life was precious and only temporary. All could be lost in a single second. Sherman's work never made him a lot of money, but it did make him rich in life. His world view was charmingly simply - Obey God, give your best in all you do, serve others in love and trust God in all circumstances. Everything else will take care of itself. Even after the tragic loss of his family, he gained a strong faith that maintained an optimism that inspired others and always pointed to Christ.

Valen cradled his friend in his arms and cried. Questions flooded his mind. The confusion, insane rage, despair and pain were too much to handle. Valen once again, knew the painful isolation of loss and was tempted to reject the truth he knew.

Then, suddenly, a shiver ran up spine, as he felt someone approaching from behind.

"So, what happened to your po' crazy man?" a chilling voice whispered.

Valen turned around slowly, horror and anger ran through him.

Jed with three of his friends stood smiling. They surrounded Valen.

Disgusted at the thought of what must have happened, Valen immediately put the puzzle together. Sherman was probably minding his own business, about to settle down for dinner, when these punks crept up behind him.

Valen stood silent as rage filled his veins.

"You know, it's a shame that old man didn't put up more of a fight. I thought he would've at least known some combat moves." Jed snickered.

Valen screamed as he lunged toward Jed. The other three guys quickly grabbed him. "I'm going to kill you! I'm gonna kill you!"

"I don't think so Valen. I think it's you whose gonna get hurt. You see, I know how to get away with just about anything. It's called brains. Something you ain't got," he said poking Valen's head. "So, you see my friend, it's you who's going to lose everything."

Jed walked up to Valen and put his face next to his. Valen could feel his hot breath against his ear. "You messed with the wrong guy, you worthless piece of trailer trash. I'm going to end you like I did your loony friend. You don't mess with me," Jed jerked

Valen by the hair. "You got that? Now hold him," Jed ordered.

"I don't think so Jed," a voice demanded from the distance.

"Who is that? Jake? Give me a break," Jed said sarcastically. "Get out of here, and I might give you a discount on your next purchase."

"Let my brother go." Jake said calmly.

Everyone in the town knew Jake. They knew he used drugs heavily, and they knew the trouble he had been into, but they also knew not to mess with him. He simply didn't care about his life, and therefore, didn't give much for others. Jed knew he would be in trouble if he didn't do what Jake asked, but his pride kept him from giving in.

"What do you care about this for?"

"He's my brother."

"Ha! That never seemed to stop you from kicking his face in yourself."

"Yea? Well, I'm allowed to. You ain't. Now, I'm done talkin'. Leave!" He shouted as he pointed a loaded pistol in Jed's face.

Jed and the rest of his gang shuffled and mumbled to each other.

"You haven't seen the last of me," Jed shouted at Valen as he strutted off. "I can promise you that!"

Jake looked at Valen for the first time since they were boys with sympathetic eyes.

"You okay?"

"Yea, I'm fine." Valen turned back toward Sherman.

"How's the old man?" Jake asked.

"He's gone."

Jake didn't say much more, things were getting a little too emotional for him. So, he decided it was time for him to leave.

"I'm sorry, Valen," Jake spoke softly.

Valen didn't say a word, and he didn't ask how his brother knew he was there

Just then Jake stopped, and turned back around. He rested his hand on Valen's shoulder. "Get out of this town. They'll eat you alive here, and you've got too much going for you. You got something special, Valen. It's something I can't understand, but I see it. Everyone sees it."

Valen looked up at his brother. He had never heard such compassion. Such sincerity. He couldn't believe it was his brother.

"Just get out," he said again.

Valen watched him walk back to his old pick-up truck, light a cigarette and skid off leaving a cloud of dust. Valen never saw Jake again.

Valen knew his brother was right, but he had more important matters to attend to at the moment. He had to give Sherman a proper burial. The burial he deserved. Valen contacted the local funeral grounds where Sherman's family was buried and they came to pick up the body.

He received a veteran's burial and most of the people Sherman had helped and cared for during his life showed up. A few people shared publicly how Sherman had impacted their lives. All were sad, but also rejoiced in knowing Sherman was finally home and reunited with his family he loved so dear, never to face pain, or hardship again.

Afterward, Valen went in detail with the cops, telling them about the murder and who the suspects were. However, despite the public sentiment, Valen could tell there wasn't much concern from the police. They were unsure about Sherman anyway. For years, the other half of the town were fearful of him and were glad to be rid of him. They never knew the kindness and only drew assumptions from his appearance, and appearances in Sherman's case were grossly misleading.

Valen left with his heart aching and disgusted. The loss and tragedy of the situation was impossible to comprehend. None of it made sense and he felt as though his emotions were driving him insane.

Valen knew he had to leave. There was nothing for him anymore, nothing but Rhiannon. He needed her. He wanted to hold her forever. He wanted to provide for her, but more than anything else, he wanted to love her. He wanted to give her all the love he never had the chance to express. He wanted to give her the world. He knew what he needed, but he was unsure if she felt the same.

Rhiannon had returned home after the funeral, but Valen ached for her comforting presence. So he sped off to find her. When he reached the front gates, he rang the buzzer. "I'm sorry to disturb you, but I was wandering if Rhiannon was available."

"Who is this?"

"Valen, sir."

"Valen? I don't know any Valen." the voice said rudely, "Now get off my property."

Valen was about to leave when Elizabeth's voice came over the speaker.

"Valen? Are you okay?"

"I'm fine, m'am. I just really needed to talk to Rhiannon."

In the background, Valen could hear Mrs. Water's explaining to her husband who he was.

"Hold on dear," Elizabeth replied. "I'll let you in and get Rhiannon."

"Thank you, Mrs. Waters."

Just as the gate was opening, Pete's voice came over the speaker again.

"So, you're the white trash whose been tryin' to get with Rhian. Well, let me tell ya' somethin', you're not even close to being good enough for her and probably never will. So, why don't you just forget it, and go back where you came from."

Valen, didn't bother to respond. He just went up the drive. All he cared about was seeing Rhiannon.

Rhiannon met Valen at the door. Mrs. Waters was there too.

"Are you okay Valen?" Rhiannon asked.

"Yea, I'm fine. I apologize for waking everyone up, Mrs. Waters."

"It's okay, hon. I know what you did for Rhiannon. I think the least I can do is open a gate for you. And I'm so sorry to hear about your friend." And with that, she headed back up the stairs. When she got to the room, she found Pete standing there, pretending that he wasn't ease dropping.

"What's that piece of trash doing in my house?" he demanded.

"So, now it's your house. I'll remind you that Cane built this home. You had no part in, and I'm allowed to let anyone I want inside."

Pete quickly backed off like the spineless coward he was. "You're right dear. I'm sorry. Come on, let's go back to bed."

Elizabeth knew the kind of man Pete was, but it was too late now. If she left him, he would try to take everything. All she could do was brush it off and accept what she had rushed in to and settled for.

Rhiannon pulled Valen in the den. "Now, tell me what's going on? Are you okay?"

"I believe Jed murdered Sherman."

"What? Are you sure?"

"Yes - I know he did. He practically told me so."

"Valen, we have to do something!"

"There's nothing to do."

"Tell the police or something!" she said desperately.

"I did, but nothing will be done. Believe me. If anyone wants to do something, it's me, but there really is nothing I can even do." Rhiannon heard the pain in Valen's voice. "They'll never tie this to Jed."

"Well, we have to try. We can't let him get away with this."

"He already has Rhiannon. This is over. His judgement will come at another time."

"Valen." Rhiannon placed her hand on his face and pulled him close, holding him tight.

"I'm so sorry."

Valen laid his head on her shoulder. All he could do was cry.

"Rhiannon." Valen said as he pulled away. "I need to leave this place."

"Why? Valen I don't understand all this," Rhiannon said confused.

"There's nothing for me here. The only thing that is keeping me here now is you."

Rhiannon stood silent with her head hung low. Thoughts raced through her mind. There were many questions, but she felt

Valen's strength and felt confident that he knew what he was doing. However, she couldn't stand the idea of him leaving.

"But what about school?"

Valen snickered lightly. "I hardly go now."

"Yea, but we're about to graduate soon." Rhiannon pleaded.

"I know. I'll probably finish school, but I don't think I'll stay much past that."

Rhiannon stood back in thought. She couldn't imagine being without Valen. She knew that just after these past few days she loved him.

"I know you need to be alone. I just put a lot on you. I'll call you tomorrow, okay?"

Rhiannon nodded. Slowly, Valen leaned over and kissed her gently on the forehead as he turned to leave. As he looked back, Rhiannon caught his eye. "I love you," she said.

"I love you too," he said as Rhiannon shut the door.

Valen didn't want to go home. There was too much going on, and for some reason, he didn't want to see his brother. It felt too awkward. He wouldn't know how to act. Would he sit beside Jake and start conversation, or ignore him like he used to do?

So, instead, Valen rode back to the spot he and Rhiannon had been the other night.

So many thoughts stormed his brain. He had to sit and try to sort them all out. His best friend just died, or was killed; and his brother, who used to abuse him, just saved his life, and now, he was faced with losing Rhiannon, again. Plus, where was he going to go?

Valen realized that before he found a place to go, he had to figure out what he wanted to do. All these questions boggled his mind. He began to appreciate Sherman's philosophy of living simply and trusting God even more. All this thinking of tomorrow was driving him crazy. Valen grabbed his head between his knees and squeezed his eyes tight trying to slow his mind, but his memories kept turning to his lost friend. And through tears and laughter he began to pray, recalling one of his favorite verses that commands us to not worry about tomorrow, for today has enough to deal with on its own.

The next day, Valen went over to see Rhiannon. This time, the gate was open, but Pete waited outside."

"So, how's it goin' boy?" Pete asked coyly.

"I'm fine, sir. Is Rhiannon available?" Valen asked, ignoring Pete's tone.

"Available for what?" he asked with a perverted grin.

"To speak with, sir." Valen was getting fed up with this guy.

Pete, sensing Valen's frustration, walked up close as if to whisper.

"Don't ya' think she's gotta nice figure for her age?" he hissed.

Valen, disgusted at this point was tempted to throw a punch, but instead, he backed away. "I wouldn't know," he snapped in reply.

"Sure you would, but let me remind you. You ain't her type.

You're a poor boy. You ain't worth much around here. You're a bastard child, and you ain't worth a nothin'. So, quit wasting your time. Rhiannon could never be with someone like you, and you know it."

Valen just looked straight into his eyes, and clenched his fists tight. "May I see Rhiannon?" he said calmly. Then, from the corner of his eye, he saw Rhiannon racing down the porch stairs.

"Valen!"

Valen turned away, as if Pete wasn't even there. "Hey Rhian! It's good to see you. I know it sounds crazy, but I feel like I haven't seen you for days."

"I know, me too."

Rhiannon pulled Valen away from her step-dad and whispered in his ear.

"Is everything okay?"

"Yea, everything's fine. I'm getting better. Thanks."

"How 'bout with Pete...I know that he can be a real pain when he wants to."

"Na, everything's fine."

The two continued their walk out to the floral garden in the back yard.

"Rhiannon?"

"Yes, Valen?"

"I was hoping you'd come with me when I leave." Valen urged.

"I know. I've been thinking about what you told me...and I want to be with you, but you know we need to finish school, and I want to go to college and then law school, and...I just still have a lot I want to do and that I'm responsible for. I hope you can understand."

Valen stood silent, feeling foolish. "I know, and I'm going to finish school too...and maybe college. I just don't know. All I know is that I've wanted to be with you as long as I can remember, and now that we're together, I don't want to lose you."

"We don't have to loose each other," Rhiannon said excitedly. "You do well in school, and without even trying. I bet you could get in and maybe a scholarship too. We can stay together!"

"Maybe," he said softly. "You know, I didn't even think of that."

"I know." Rhiannon smiled.

"I guess I could try. It wouldn't hurt." Valen said.

"Yea!" Rhiannon shouted. "I know it can work out."

"Okay!" Valen smiled. "I'll do it!"

"Really?" Rhiannon couldn't believe her ears. "That's great! I'll help you send in all the papers," she said throwing her arms around his neck. "Oh, I love you to death!"

"I love you, too." Valen sighed. He couldn't believe what he just committed too.

What was at college for him? He wanted to go somewhere far

from this town – far from where he was. He wanted to be where no one knew him - maybe New York, or even California. He wanted to see the world now, not put it off, but he didn't want to lose this woman in his life either. She made him feel, connected and whole.

Valen wanted to make his living doing what he loved, like writing and photography - but how? He had never been published before, and besides, his writing didn't appear to be the caliber other's would appreciate. He didn't even know if he was any good. All of his writings were for self-gratification, no one else's. Sherman hadn't even read one of his works.

Valen's photographs were a different story all together - he knew they were good. In fact, he had won several awards for a few of his black and white photos in school competitions. Valen had a gift at being able to capture the communication of life - the moment. One photo, displayed in the school's art studio, was of two men talking on a park bench. One of the men was homeless, wearing old, tattered clothes. The other was a well-dressed professor. Both men were debating their differing viewpoints on religion and war. Valen had joined in the conversation earlier and was able to take a candid photo during one of the more heated moments of conversation. He actually captured their words and emotions. It was amazing. One could almost hear their conversation through the picture.

So, Valen knew what he would like to do, but could he make a living at it? And a good living at that? For even though he was drawn to doing what he loved, he was also driven by the lure of money.   And pursing an artistic career usually meant going without, for at least awhile, and he was sick of going without. He wanted more. He wanted respect.

Days passed and soon Rhiannon received all the papers Valen needed to begin applying to various schools.

Valen loved Rhiannon, he truly did, but he wasn't sure of how things were moving. He knew he wanted to be with her, even marry her, but he had to find himself first. He had to find some inner peace and comfort, before he could settle down and be good for anyone else. Something inside him just wasn't at peace. He missed Sherman's council. He needed some wisdom and someone to talk to about his upcoming decisions, but he wasn't sure where to turn.

Rhiannon on the other hand, was ecstatic about the whole thing. She knew she wanted Valen, but could sense his hesitation. However, she didn't want to acknowledge her intuitions, so she ignored them.

Finally, graduation day came and surprisingly, even though he hadn't attended many of his classes, Valen received his diploma. When his name was called however, there was a strange reaction. Hardly any applause was heard, only the small hands of Rhiannon's clapping stood out. The silence was deafening.

Rhiannon's acceptance was much grander. A giant roar could be heard throughout the stadium.

After graduation a bunch of the kids headed out to a party that was being held in the same clearing of the woods where Valen had first reunited with Rhiannon and confronted Jed. Valen prepared himself for an interesting night.

Jed nudged his buddies at the site of Valen's arrival and smiled his crooked grin.

"Well, look who it is, Mr. Pansy himself. Don't you know freaks ain't wanted here. I mean, no one even clapped for you today. You're a loser - figure it out!"

Rhiannon grabbed Valen's clenched fist and nudged him to walk away, but Valen knew this had to be settled. He knew Jed killed Sherman, whether by accident, or on purpose, and he knew that Jed was the kind of guy whose pride would get the best of him. Jed wasn't about to let anyone tarnish his reputation, especially someone on the "outside" like Valen.

Valen's eyes met Jed's. Both glared hatred. "What? You want some of me?" Jed defended.

"Yea, I do." Valen said, never breaking eye contact.

Jed pushed Valen against a tree. "Com'on then! Com'on!"

Valen looked at Rhiannon who was in fear of what was to come. Noticing Valen's gaze towards Rhiannon, Jed went and grabbed her by the hair.

"Hey Val? Is she tasty or what?" He said as he ran his tongue over her cheek.

Without a second's hesitation Valen's hands were around Jed's throat. Jed's arms flapped all around, as he gasped for air. Rhiannon, kneeling on the ground, trembled with fear. This time, she wasn't going to stop Valen.

Rage fueled his body, and all the pain Jed had caused him erupted in his mind. "I'm gonna kill you!" he stated as he rammed in his knee into Jed's stomach, never once letting go of his throat.

No one tried to stop the fight. The energy could be felt in the air, and no one wanted to get involved. They watched quietly, everyone, just watched. Nothing could be heard, but Jed's gasping for air, and Valen stood there, without expression, slowly draining the life from Jed's body.

Then, a voice broke the silence, it was, Rhiannon. "Valen, don't!" She cried. "You have too much. Please don't blow it on him. He's not worth it. Please!"

Valen turned to see the tears in Rhiannon's eyes and her concern for him. Slowly, he released his grip.

Jed panted for air, and his eyes filled with tears. He knew how close he got to death. Coldness filled his veins.

Rhiannon grabbed Valen's arm. "Come on. Let's go. It is over Valen. Let's just go."

As Valen turned, Jed reached into his boot and pulled out a gun. Then, just as he was taking aim, one of his cronies grabbed his hand. "Don't do it, Jed. This one's over."

As Valen and Rhiannon rode off, Valen felt something in him change.

"Where are we going Valen?"

"I don't know. Let's just ride."

The next morning found them lying in each other's arms by the lake cliff they had visited earlier.

"Oh, no. It's 6 a.m. My mom is going to kill me! Rhiannon screamed.

"We have to go."

When they got to Rhiannon's house, her mom raced out to meet them.

"Where have you been? Get inside right now!"

"I'm sorry Mrs. Waters, it's my fault, I...."

"I don't want to hear from you. I don't want to see you. I trusted you, Valen. God knows why, but I did. I don't want you seeing Rhiannon any more. Do you hear me? No more!"

Valen sat stunned, and watched as Pete approached wearing a sly grin.

"I thought I told you that you don't belong here. You never did. Now get off my property before I call the cops."

Valen, too tired to fight, didn't feel like wasting his time on this guy. Too much had already happened, and he just needed some time to himself. So, without a word, he cranked his bike and began pulling away.

"Oh, Valen!" Pete stated. "I'll be sure to give Rhiannon a special kiss for you tonight," he winked.

Valen immediately stopped his bike and looked him right in the eye. "If you touch her," he said assuredly. "you'll regret it." And with that, he rode away.

That night, at home, Valen couldn't slow his mind. So, he turned to the only release he knew - writing. He pulled out his old ragged notebook and began pouring his heart into it. He wrote about Sherman, Jed, his brother, Pete and Rhiannon. He wrote about them all, and he came to one conclusion. It was time to leave it all. There was too much pain and loss. He had to leave and pursue his dream, but even more, he had to find himself. To do that, he had to leave Rhiannon. She was his heart, and it tore at his soul to leave her, but he knew it was the right decision.

Sadly, even though he knew God and accepted Jesus, he had not fully surrendered and his life was being torn. He hadn't fully realized the power and freedom Christ offered. So, he strained with the restlessness that exists in the lukewarm in-between.

Early the next morning, a pounding at the door interrupted Valen's thoughts. It was Rhiannon, and she was soaking wet with sweat. She had run all the way from her house.

"Rhiannon? What's wrong? What happened? Are you okay?"

She tried to speak, but was out of breath. Valen led her to the couch and caressed her hair until she calmed down. "It's okay, just tell me what happened."

"It's my step-dad," she panted, "he..." Rhiannon shook in disgust.

"What, Rhiannon? What happened?" Valen asked calmly.

"Well, at first I didn't think much about it, but..." she paused in thought.

"But what, Rhiannon?" Valen continued, stroking her hair.

"He walked in on me while I was in the bathroom. I didn't think - I mean, I didn't lock the door, but now when I think about the look he gave me..."

"Did he try to touch you?"

Rhiannon looked down and seemed embarrassed. "No."

"He didn't touch you."

"No."

"So, what happened."

"It's hard to explain. All I know is that he gave me a real funny feeling, because later he came in my room and sat on my bed. It just gave me the creeps, Valen," she said in tears.

Valen put his arm around her and held her close. "I know, but you're okay. Thank, God. You did the right thing." Valen rocked her in his arms and she fell asleep. He laid her down and let her rest there on the couch.

Rhiannon awoke to the aroma of pancakes and eggs. Valen had gotten up after she dozed off to start breakfast. "It smells delicious in here." she said.

"Thank you." Valen replied. " How do you like your eggs?"

"Scrambled."

"Okay, scrambled it is," as he broke eggs in the skillet.

Rhiannon jumped on the counter next to him.

"I love you, Valen," she whispered.

"I love you too."

Rhiannon's face suddenly got somber, and she jumped back down. "I've been thinking."

"About what?" Valen said as he chopped at the eggs.

"I don't think it's fair to ask you to come with me to college. You have your own life, your own dreams, and I don't think you'd be happy there."

Valen turned down the heat to the stove and faced Rhiannon's tear-filled eyes.

"Rhiannon, what are you saying?"

"I know you don't want to come, and it's okay. I don't think you should."

Valen couldn't believe what he was hearing. "Rhian, I love you. That's all that matters. I can write and take pictures wherever I am. As long as I'm with you, I'm happy."

Valen meant what he said, but inside there was still a struggle, and Rhiannon could sense it. She knew he loved her, but felt their paths were different.

Rhiannon was hoping the old philosophy was true, that if you love something, and let it go, it will come back if it's true love and meant to be.

Neither had yet learned true love was commitment and sacrificial. It was all based on emotion, at this point, and although they knew God, they had not yet placed Him central in their decisions. He was still residing on the peripheral of their lives.

"I know you love me, Valen, and you know I love you more than anything else in my life, but things have been real crazy around here the past few days, and it's all happened so fast. I just don't want you to make any sacrifices you may regret down the road. Do you understand what I'm trying to say?" Rhiannon took his hand.

"Yes, I do, and I appreciate your thoughtfulness, but I'm telling you, it's us that I want."

Valen held her close and knew what she said was right. They had to go their separate ways. Valen's heart ached at the thought of losing her.

"I don't know if I can bare being without you, Rhiannon. You're my soul. How can I be without you?"

"If this is meant to be, we will be. I believe that," she smiled.

"What about your step-dad? How are you going to deal with him?"

"He's just a pervert, Valen. He's a wimp and a sissy, who's afraid of losing my mother's money. He won't do anything. I know that. He definitely gives me the creeps, and I'm going to tell my mother what he did. It won't happen again, because I'm not going to keep quiet about it."

Valen knew what she said was true, and also knew Pete was a coward. He was a big talker that hid behind falsehoods. However, he still worried. Valen placed his hands around her face. "I love you, Rhiannon. I always will, and I'm going to marry you. I promise you that."

Rhiannon looked to the floor and began to cry. She held him tightly. Valen lifted her head by her chin and kissed her softly. Rhiannon knew she had to go.

The next day, Valen ached for Rhiannon, but he knew she had already gone her way and it was time for him to go his. As he began packing, he found a note she had left in his drawer with a single yellow rose she had picked from the yard.

Valen didn't have to read the note, he knew what it said, but his curiosity got the best of him. So, he sat on the side of the bed, took a deep breath and prepared for more heartache.

"Dear Valen,

You are the most beautiful person in the world. Your dreams give me inspiration, and your heart gives me hope. For the time we've known each other, you've changed my life. I now know what true love is. It's sacrifice.

Leaving you is the hardest thing I've ever had to do, and I hate myself for it, but I feel it's best for both of us. Our paths are taking us different directions. You're the dreamer, full of imagination and fantasy. You keep me true. I believe in your dreams, and I know you'll succeed in all your endeavors.

At the same time, I have to pursue mine. I have always wanted to be a lawyer. I don't know why, Valen, but I have; and I know I'll be a good one. I feel I can make a difference. It's just something I have to do. I know you understand.

We must believe that if we are meant to be, and that God brought us together, then we'll find each other again someday, but if for some reason we don't, I'll cherish our memory forever. You live in my heart, Valen. Thank you for all we've shared.

I love you.

Rhiannon"

Valen folded the letter back, neatly and put it away in an old metal box he kept by his bed. Inside the box, the letter joined an old photograph of his parents and a fishing lure of Sherman's.

The time to go had finally come, and it didn't take long to pack. There was nothing for him there anymore, and other than the box and a few crumbled up clothes, he left it all behind. After tying everything on his bike, Valen took one last look back, smiled and drove off to find his new life. Once again neglecting to seek God in the process.

Highways End

Chapter VI

Valen rode without cause and without direction. In fact, he didn't even know where he was going first. He was just going to let the cards fall where they may and follow his instincts.

Along the way he'd stop to take pictures of what he saw and wrote of what he experienced. He felt what he thought was freedom - and what a feeling! He drove with the wind in his hair, and with the voice of nature around him. He was going to where his destiny led him, and it felt good for the moment.

Rhiannon was following what she felt was her destiny as well. She rode with her mom up to Atlanta and enrolled in her pre-law classes. She knew what she wanted to be and was taking her first step to get there.

Although Valen and Rhiannon's paths were different, and took them far from each other, they never lost hope. Their love was stronger than ever, and every free thought was spent on the other.

They were out to make their own mark. They were young, foolish, stubborn and strong. Their minds were fresh and on fire with dreams, but most importantly, they believed in their dreams and that they were possible.

Rhiannon aced all her courses, and was the leading law student in her class. Potential internship offers were even being made before her final year of school was over.

She was also maturing to be more beautiful than ever. She gained the look of experience, and her eyes glazed with determination. She was aggressive, charming and rarely lost at anything she went for. Needless to say, men were attracted, in particular, another law student named, Josh Malk.

Josh was also charming, but devilish. He was also quite handsome and knew it. He had soft, flowing blonde hair that seemed to glisten in the sunlight, and his eyes were steel blue. He had a smile that stretched from ear to ear and his teeth sparkled in perfect form. It was as if Prince Charming himself stepped out of the storybooks.

Rhiannon, like most women, was enticed by his charms. He had rehearsed all the lines of a gentleman and could play the part well. Rhiannon would tell him stories of Valen and of their time together, and Josh would listen. He knew the way to a woman's heart was by listening. So, Rhiannon began to trust his friendship, and they began to spend more and more time together. They had an independent relationship however, and Josh would let Rhiannon pick-up their dinner tab whenever possible.

Josh's specialization was tax law, and he had been studying it now for several years. He was taking his time, and why not, it was a good line to say you were in law school. He could even be a long-term living off mom and dad student while gaining the admiration of family and friends at the same time. In return, his parents had bragging rights and relished the opportunity to tell their friends their son was in law school. So, it was a win - win situation.

Valen on the other hand, continued going at it alone and spent his days pursuing a career as an artist. He had driven all the way to New York, thinking that was the place he needed to be in order for his expression to be understood. However, instead, he was more like a fish out of water. New York was a much faster life than he was used to. The people there weren't rude, they were just serious and always in a hurry to get somewhere. Valen just couldn't keep up with the pace.

Valen's photographs weren't accepted in New York either. Instead, photos with a more abstract outlook seemed to gain the most recognition. So, obviously, his captured moments of human interaction were mostly rejected. His writing was even shunned, and he began losing hope in his dream of ever becoming a reality.

Valen knew almost instantly that New York was not the place for him. He had to go someplace a little more familiar, someplace where life moved at a pace more his style.

Rhiannon of course was in her element and graduated from law school in record time. Many of the top law firms were sending her offers. Rhiannon was at the top of her game and was exactly where she had always wanted to be. Her final decision was to join a well-respected international law firm there in Atlanta.

Josh on the other hand, remained in school, and eventually tired of the fast pace Rhiannon chose to live. Several years had passed now, and he and Rhiannon were now more like old acquaintances. He was too busy enjoying the college life and she was too busy climbing the corporate ladder. The final closure to their relationship however, came one night at a party that he lured her into going to.

"Com'on," he begged. "You are working too hard and need a break. We'll have fun. You'll see."

"I really can't. I have to get some paper work done before

tomorrow night's staff meeting."

"Ah, you'll be fine. Now, com'on," he smiled as he pulled her out the door.

Rhiannon followed unenthusiastically.

The club was actually one of the calmer locations Josh visited, but for Rhiannon it was still too much.

"Josh!" she yelled over the pounding music. Josh's face rose from the glass of beer it was buried in. "Josh!" she repeated.

"What?" he replied, suddenly noticing the blonde sitting to his right.

"I want to go home," Rhiannon shouted.

"What? Now? Why? The party's just gettin' started."

"I'm tired, and I have to get some work done tomorrow. Now, take me home." Rhiannon burned a gaze of disgust right through him.

"Okay, calm down, we'll go," Josh said stumbling to the door.

Rhiannon reached out her hand. "Give me your keys. I'm driving."

"But of course my dear." Josh slurred as he dug into his pocket for the keys.

By the time they made it home, Josh was practically passed out.

"Are we there yet?" he slurred.

"Yes, thank God, and I'm going to bed." Rhiannon sighed. "You can sleep on the couch."

Josh rolled his eyes as a child would to his mother and slammed himself into the cushions of the couch. He passed out instantly.

As Rhiannon changed for bed, she thought about her life and where it was going, and she wondered what Valen was doing. The thought of him taking pictures and writing poetry somewhere made her smile. She hoped he was happy.

The next morning came early, and Rhiannon tiptoed around so not to wake Josh, who was drooling all over himself. She was disgusted by his appearance now and couldn't believe she had ever fallen victim to his charms. She was ashamed that she had ever let him hold her, but was proud that she never allowed herself to go any further. She still held on to the dream of saving herself for her husband. A position she knew many considered outdated, but something she knew was right.

By 7 AM, Rhiannon was dressed and at the office busy returning calls and organizing her day. There were old cases to file and new clients to see. Most of Rhiannon's days were rushed and hectic, but she had learned to live with the stress. In fact, she needed it to keep her going and inspired. Being the bright new kid in the firm was a challenge, but every day was fun for her. However, somewhere deep inside, she was still empty and bored.

She was bored with all her fellow lawyers' egos. She was bored with the clients that were only looking for a quick buck, and she was bored with her routine. Although she appeared to have almost everything a person could want - a promising career, money and a good-looking man waiting in her apartment, she was not satisfied.

She was doing what she wanted and enjoyed her job. So, why was she still unhappy? She felt guilty for feeling that way. After all, she had no reason to be sad. She had it all. Perhaps she was too much of a dreamer. She had discovered that there were more things she wanted to do, not just law. Her interests were growing and her curiosities expanding.

The schedule she lived by was hectic and taking its toll. She was tired of fighting traffic every day and with how the majority of her time was being spent. She felt as though her life was moving in a circle and not forward. All she did was work, eat and sleep; and she knew there was more to life than that.

Immediately, her memory shot back to Valen. Her mind drifted, and she trembled as the memories they shared flooded back to her. She would love to see him again, but had no idea as to where he was. There was nothing she could do but put on a smile and plan for her future.

She thought about other things she could do. She had worked hard to get where she was, and she was good at law. Rhiannon strained to calm her mind with the wild thoughts of pursuing other dreams. Law was all she knew. The money was good, the work was honest and she was doing a good service. So, like so many others do, Rhiannon continued with her career, buried herself in a comfort zone and disallowed herself to think about fulfilling any of those crazy thoughts she had floating in her head. She convinced herself that she had to be realistic.

Rhiannon sighed when she returned home and saw Josh's car still parked outside. All she really wanted to do was play some soft music, and sit in the dark by candlelight, but now, instead, she had to entertain this kid.

Upon entering the door Rhiannon decided she was going to end the relationship once and for all. Taking a deep breath, she mustered up some courage and walked in, but to her surprise Josh wasn't there. In fact, all the lights were out. In the distance, she thought she heard voices. Straining, she noticed they were coming from the bedroom.

Rhiannon opened the door slowly and to her disgust, saw a woman in her bed. Shocked, Josh rolled out from the covers and stumbled to the floor. "You're early," was all he could think to say.

Rhiannon looked to the ground and just laughed in disgust. "You bum," she said. "You have some serious nerve bringing this into my apartment!" Rhiannon's eyes shot back to the woman who was modestly picking her clothes off the floor.

"Get out of my apartment...Get out!"

The girl quickly threw on her shirt and ran out the door.

"Now," Rhiannon directed her attention back to Josh. "Leave."

"But, Rhiannon, you don't understand. You're over-reacting, really. I swear, I'm sorry. Please let me explain." Again, all Rhiannon could do was laugh.

"No, Josh, there's nothing to explain. I don't know what took me this long to realize the kind of person you are. Now get out."

"Rhiannon, you don't understand! Don't do this!" Josh begged.

"Josh, you're pathetic, and honestly, I'm bored with you. So, just leave, before you make a bigger fool of yourself."

Josh knew he wasn't going to be able to get out of this one. So, with all expression lost in his face, he got dressed, threw on his hat and walked out, closing the door softly behind him.

Chapter VII

Although Valen was not accepted in New York, he didn't give up. Every day, he looked around and wondered why he was there. His run-down apartment was in the worst side of town, and he was having trouble making his rent. The only jobs he could find were waiting tables at night. The tips were good though. Many nights, old rich women would slip hundred-dollar bills in his pockets. He of course would smile and flirt graciously. One night in particular, a regular guest of the restaurant stopped by to proposition him. She wondered if he needed a place to stay. Valen knew what she wanted, but he turned her down with a thank you and kiss on the cheek.

Living in poverty in New York had a way of testing his morals. It was very easy to sell out and do things he normally wouldn't do. Again, Valen knew he was in the wrong place. He felt his creativity and goals begin to diminish, and he began to doubt his talents as a writer. It was time to leave.

So, Valen packed his small gym bag with his belongings and left New York. This time, he headed back south. On the road, Valen's imagination began to soar once more. He knew he was heading in the right direction.

Valen thought how great it was, that whenever he got low, or discouraged, he could hop on his bike for a drive, and all would be well.

The miles flew by as Valen raced down the road. All he could think was how beautiful everything was. The tall swaying pines, the gently sloping mountaintops and the whispering streams. He was amazed at the beauty around him - at times, it all seemed so overwhelming and hard to take in.

Occasionally, Valen would stop to enjoy a sunset, or to rinse off in a nearby stream. To Valen, this was like heaven. He had his imagination to keep him company, nature for conversation and his bike for travel. He felt at peace, but still something remained missing in his heart - he wished Rhiannon was by his side.

One night, Valen decided to drive off the road a little ways and find a campsite. He found it under a big southern oak. Spanish moss hung thick across its limbs, and its trunk seemed 10 feet wide. It was a natural work of art, and Valen could almost smell its history. The times it lived through, the generations that had touched its branches - Valen stood silent and allowed his mind to drift.

Later that night after the soft orange sky turned to a deep purple, Valen sat against the oak and pulled out some beef jerky he had in his pack. He sat gazing upon the millions of stars above him and wondered where Rhiannon might be that night. A sudden flash of sadness and loneliness hit him. He missed her. She was truly the one thing he needed in his life, but she was busy with other things. He was sure that she loved him, but was afraid she had forgotten him. Valen pulled out a small pad he kept in his back pocket and started scribbling the words flowing from his heart. Satisfied and relieved with his feelings now released on paper, he drifted off to sleep.

The next day was hot and sticky. Southern summer was in full force. Valen rolled his old dirty blanket up and tied it to the back of his bike and was back on the road. He still hadn't the slightest idea as to where he was going, but knew he was heading in the right direction.

Again, Valen's mind raced with ideas. He couldn't wait to get started once more in making his dream a reality. He thought of how he could do it and the best way to get it started. He didn't want to make the same mistakes he made in New York. One of the obvious lessons learned was focus. He had to stay committed and couldn't allow himself to drift. There was still the problem of money though. Hopefully, he would be able to sell his work to a new audience.

The miles continued to pass and time began to escape him. Bewildered with thought, Valen pulled off the road and into a gas station. With all the daydreaming, he had barely noticed that he was almost out of gas.

Two old men sat outside the station on a bench watching cars go by. It was their daily routine. "Howdy," Valen said as he unscrewed the cap off his tank. The old men just nodded in response.

"Hot day. You think we might get some rain to cool things off?" Valen asked.

"Na, thangs have been dry for a while. Need some tho," one of the men responded, smacking his gums.

Valen chuckled inside himself at the simplicity of the two men and was somewhat jealous at the peace he assumed they knew.

The man that had spoken to Valen was now in the process of rolling a cigarette. He was wearing an old cowboy hat and had skin as wrinkled as worn leather. He reminded Valen of the

Marlboro Man aged forty years. The old man's hands shook as he carefully lifted the cigarette to lick it closed. The gentleman to his left, a bit younger, but still old, graced him with a light.

The two men looked like brothers in a rugged sort of way. The other gentleman was wearing a John Deere hat and was dressed in denim from head to toe. His boots were covered with dried mud.

Valen screwed the cap back on his tank and walked towards the store to pay his bill. He was thirsty and needed a cold drink.

"Y'all sell beer here?" He asked.

"That's all we sell, son," the man on his left responded in a coughing laugh.

Inside, the store looked as though it was straight out of the old west. Dusty wood floors and walls lined with bent metal Coca-Cola advertisements. Valen went to the large barrel filled with ice and pulled out a frost-covered beer. His mouth watered with anticipation.

The guy with the muddy boots walked in to attend the register.

"That be all?" he asked.

"Yes, sir. This and eight dollars-worth of gas." Valen placed the beer on the counter.

"Ten nineteen," the old man demanded.

Valen laid eleven on the table, and popped the top off the beer. "Thank ya', sir." He said as he put the beer to his lips. It was ice cold and stung as it went down, but it felt good. Or, at least he had convinced himself it felt good.

"Where ya headin' son, you look like you might be lost. I haven't seen ya 'round here before." The old man queried.

Valen thought to himself for a while because he wasn't sure where he was going, but oddly enough he didn't feel lost.

"Well, sir, I don't rightly know, but I'm sure I'm headin' in the right direction." Valen smiled.

The old man looked at Valen with understanding eyes, and smiled as if he'd been there before. "That so? Well, good luck to ya."

Valen nodded in appreciation and finished his beer with one long gulp.

Back outside, Valen struggled with his bike until he finally got it started. Before he left, he glanced at the two men and wished for the nerve to just sit and talk with them. He was curious as to where they had been and what brought them to where they were now. He felt an odd familiarity with the two men, but instead of starting a conversation, he drove off.

It seemed that the longer Sherman was dead, the farther he was drifting from God and back to his old concerns. His old thoughts and his old struggles. He looked to others and wondered about their appearance of peace and he hungered for the same, but he had forgotten where to look. Or, he was choosing not to look where he knew he should. So, he kept looking out to the world.

Almost instantly, his mind drifted back into imagination. He pictured himself on the ocean's shore, listening to waves gently crashing over rocks and sand. He dreamed of sailing on a boat and manning the mast. He could almost feel the cool misty water against his face.

Valen was a dreamer and full of imagination, but he didn't want to knock them off just as fantasies. So, he struggled to figure out how he could make all of his dreams a reality. He wanted to live them, not just dream them. That's when he decided to head for the ocean.

Now having a direction, Valen thought of what he could do to make some money and sell his work. Unfortunately, he knew he'd have to get another job waiting tables to pay the bills for a while.

Like most people, Valen wanted to make a living doing what he loved, but the fact of having to work at something you can't stand in order to do what you love was aggravating. Conflicting thoughts bombarded his mind. Only a small percentage actually make a living doing what they love, and those that do are usually extremely lucky – no way, they make their luck! He re-thought.

Valen held to a belief that you can do anything you put your mind to and work hard to achieve. He also felt that work could be a passion and source of enjoyment, but at the same time, he kept hearing in his mind the old saying his brother used to say, "If work was fun, it wouldn't be a four letter word called work."

So, there was the internal struggle. Can one have it all? Can you do what you love and make a living at it? Or, should one even care?

These questions haunted Valen and teased his brain for he had lost everything he had ever known. Happiness was foreign and pain was something he was comfortable with. He almost felt something must be wrong if everything was right in his life. So, he struggled to overcome this disturbing psyche. He wanted to believe in his talents and overcome his fear that there was no hope for his writings, or photographs.

The fear was discouraging, but the thought of being a waiter forever was even worse. Valen needed to believe in his dreams for strength and for a feeling of purpose. So, he decided to quit questioning himself. He would just do it. He knew he could make his life the way he wanted it. After all, it was his life, not someone else's. And he knew that if he wasn't doing what he loved, he wouldn't be living his life to the fullest. He needed to chase his dreams - that was living to him. He wasn't going to allow himself to be beat down by life, and he wasn't going to simply survive. He was going to fight for what he wanted, and if he failed, at least he failed trying."

A smile filled his face as he drove, and for a moment, his mind was at rest.

Valen reached the coast the following day. He was broke, tired and hungry. So, his first stop was to the beach, where he bedded down to take a nap.

He woke to the growling in his stomach and decided to go to the docks to look for work so that he could eat. In less than an hour's time, he was loading and unloading cargo shipments. It didn't pay much, but it provided Valen with enough money to rent out a small room in one of the dock worker's shacks and to buy some food.

It was the middle of summer and the smell at the docks was

awful. Many boats unloaded their dead cargo, and for the first couple of days of work Valen found himself running to the end of the pier to vomit. Eventually, he grew somewhat accustomed to the odor of spoiling fish, but never looked at seafood quite the same way again.

The dock worker Valen found to rent living space from was an older gentleman that smelled of whiskey. He was someone that enjoyed a drink, and wasn't afraid to admit it. However, the old man never seemed to get drunk. He always managed to conduct himself in a respectful manner. His name was Samuel Travers, and he had tattoos painted all over his body. His face looked twice his age and was covered with a trimmed, half grown beard. His hair was long and silver and was always worn in a ponytail.

Samuel's attire consisted of about three khaki pants and two light blue oxfords that he interchanged daily. All his T-shirts were stained yellow with sweat, and the only shoes he had were a worn pair of leather boots. However, with all that said, he never appeared dirty. He was always clean and made sure that even though his work and life was hard, he tried to never show it.

Every night, Valen would observe Sammy writing in his diary. What, he never knew, but Sammy never missed a day. He would huddle himself in the same corner of the room and light the same candle, religiously.

Valen found Sammy to be an extremely interesting and peculiar man who he enjoyed being around. However, they hardly spoke. The two would simply pass throughout the day, and sometimes never say a word.

The shack they shared was rather quaint. It sat on a hill just above the coast all by itself, was close to the beach and only a few miles from the docks where they both worked. The place was made of a type of wood Valen wasn't familiar with, but the smell it produced was welcoming. It was a mix between an antique store and library.

There was an old stone fireplace that Sammy doubled as a stove, even though he had a perfectly functioning one in the kitchen. He simply preferred the old fashioned way. He thought food tasted better when cooked over an open fire.

The only decoration in the home was above the fireplace. It was a black and white photograph of a young brunette woman. She had on a simple cross neckless and her eyes almost shined through the picture. The photo appeared to be very old and was wrinkling at the ends.

One night during one of Valen's attempts to start conversation, he asked Samuel who the woman was.

"It's my Aunt," he replied. "She and my mother were twins, but my mother died without me ever knowing her."

Valen nodded. "How'd she die?" he asked.

"Cancer. I was about three. My father wasn't around, so after her death, my aunt took me in. She took care of me, or did her best anyway. She was a special woman." Sammy's eyes were locked on the photo. "This photo has always comforted me. I don't know why."

Valen smiled. "I never had the chance to know my mother either. She left when I was young, but I do remember the few nights she held me as being very peaceful.

The old man smiled and with that, stood up to go to bed.

After Samuel left the room, Valen got up and walked over to the picture. The woman was beautiful. Her smile reminded him of Rhiannon's.

He tried not to think of Rhiannon too often. The thoughts always brought him sadness. Valen placed the picture back down, and walked outside to the beach. He gazed up at the sky, and found comfort in the thought that Rhiannon shared the same moon. Maybe she was looking at it now? Valen hoped so. This thought somehow brought him peace and a feeling of closeness.

Valen drifted to the days he and Rhiannon had spent together. They had shared so much in such a short time. Their love grew faster than either of them could ever have imagined. What was she doing now? Knowing Rhiannon, Valen was sure she had captured her dream. He knew she was doing what she always wanted. His only wish was that she was happy. He wanted to contact her, but his pride prevented it. He didn't want her to know how he had been spending his time. He was still poor, lost and living in a shack. He couldn't face her now. Not yet. He still had so much to accomplish. He dreamed of making his millions, and then showing up to take her away, back to their own world - their own fantasy.

The next morning, Valen woke to find himself still on the beach. He felt slimy from the salt air, and headed back to the house to wash up. Samuel was by the fireplace cooking grits. "Help yourself," he said without even looking back to acknowledge Valen's presence.

"Thank you. I think I will," Valen said modestly.

Valen grabbed a bowl from out of the sink and rinsed it clean. He walked up beside Samuel and scooped a healthy helping.

Samuel glanced at Valen in thought. "There's a big shipment expected to come in today. We should be pretty busy," he said.

"Good, I can use the work, not to mention the money," Valen responded.

Valen gulped down his breakfast, placed the bowl back in the sink, and headed to the bathroom to rinse off. When he stepped back into the den, Samuel was already gone. Valen threw on his hat and headed out to the docks.

When he got there, he noticed some commotion taking place. Valen fought his way through the crowd and saw Samuel defending off three younger men. They were part of the crew that had just sailed in, and they were still drunk from the night before.

"What's going on?" Valen asked the lady standing beside him. She was totally engrossed in the show.

"Those three men were picking on that poor old man. He had gone up to lift one of the crates, when that man there,' she pointed to the tallest man in the bunch, 'pushed him down the ramp."

"Why?" Valen asked.

"I don't know," the woman said softly.

All three men were quite large and stunk of booze and body odor. They obviously had been out awhile and were ready to create some excitement. Samuel was just at the wrong place at the wrong time. Besides that, he looked like an easy target for the men.

Valen immediately stepped in to break it up. "All right," he said, "let's break it up. You don't want to mess with some old man. Big guys like you need more of a challenge don't ya'," Valen said trying to convince the guys to go on their way.

"Oh, ain't that cute. The boy's so heroic," the men responded sarcastically. The biggest guy of the three stepped up towards Valen. He towered above him, and Valen looked like a kid next to him.

"Com'on now, I don't want any trouble. Just let us do our job and we'll be gone," Valen said as he backed up towards Samuel.

All three guys looked around at each other. "Na, I don't think so," the largest guy responded, as he came up on Valen again.

"What's going on out here?" A voice yelled from off the ship. It was the ships' Captain.

"Don! Gil! Becker! Get back up here!" he ordered. The two other men looked at the taller one for direction.

"Com'on let's go," he said smugly, knocking Valen with his shoulder as he walked by.

Valen's attention shot back to Samuel, who was bleeding heavily from the nose. "Are you okay?" he asked.

"Yea,' the old man said proudly, 'I've had to deal with guys like that my whole life. It ain't nothin,'" he said.

Slowly, the crowd began to disperse. "What was that all about?" Valen asked.

"Ahh, from time to time you have to deal with guys like that. Ain't nothin'. Com'on let's get back to work," Samuel said confidently.

Valen and Samuel headed back up the ramp and began unloading the shipment. The three guys were obviously sent down below, because they didn't show back up. The Captain, a greasy looking fellow, with deep beady eyes, didn't even bother to make condolences to Valen, or Samuel. He immediately began given orders as to which crates were to stay and which were to go.

After all cargo was unloaded, Valen and Samuel were handed their money, and asked to leave. "Com'on,' Samuel said to Valen, 'let's get a drink'." The two headed down to the local bar, just a few feet away.

In the bar, Samuel must have felt a connection, or gratitude to Valen, because as he drank, he slowly began to open up and talk of himself for the first time.

"I was an only child born in Maine and grew up poor without any male figure around. My mother was a beautifully kind woman that loved me very much. She was sick often though and as I mentioned, died of untreated breast cancer when I was just three. Anyway, that's when her twin sister, Diana, came into my life. I hadn't really known her before. She was always busy with her own life, but after my mom's death, she was the first one by my side. Within a day, she had me moved and living with her in Boston.

Diana worked as a waitress at a diner near our apartment and was gone most of the time, but she was a loving woman and took very good care of me. Whenever possible, she'd take me to baseball games, or keep me busy with other activities.

Surprisingly, I was a popular kid in school and excelled in all my classes. I was however an outspoken person and often found myself in the principal's office for disruptive behavior. Aunt Diana would always show up in her dirtied apron from work and sit through the parent - teacher sessions. She never yelled or got mad at me though. She knew I was a good kid, I guess, or maybe she never knew what to say. I don't know. All I do know is that she was always there for me. She had great faith, and was a good Christian woman.

The remainder of my youth was spent in and out of fights and working at local bars. I went to college on a scholarship and majored in journalism. However, I could never quite find a career that fit me after graduation. So, tired of the city and looking for something different, I decided to head for the beach. It's here that I took up dock work and fishing. I seem to have found myself here, and believe it or not, I find pride in what I do. There's a kinship I share with the seamen from thousands of years ago. I do what they did then. Not much has changed. The sea gives us what we need.

Valen sat and listened carefully. He was surprised at how deceiving looks could be. He would've never guessed Sam to be a college graduate that once worked in the city. Valen also wondered why Samuel never found anyone to share his life with, and he thought how lonely he must be. Sammy did however appear to have found some peace. Although a man that drank that much, could never have true peace. He was however committed to something he felt worked for him, and Valen for the moment envied him for at least having that.

As the day came to an end, the bar grew more crowded. It was filled with mostly dockworkers and fishermen with hungry thirsts, and as the night grew older, the crowd grew rougher.

Samuel tossed back his last swig of the pitcher and raised his finger to get the waitress' attention.

"Yes, sir?" she smiled flirtatiously. The young woman was working the whole room, hoping for big tips.

"Another pitcher." Samuel shouted as he lit a cigarette.

The two men then shared a brief moment of silence as they thought. Eventually, Samuel began to open up again. Valen was glad, he hadn't heard these many words from Sammy's mouth since he'd gotten to the ocean. He was enjoying the moment.

"I feel as though I can trust you, Valen, I don't know why, but I've dissected your actions and words and find you to be a sincere person - something rare in today's world filled with masks. If you know what I mean. Everyone hides their true self, even me."

"What do you mean?" Valen leaned forward with keen interest. Sam had always been so distant. So, cool. He didn't want to miss this moment.

"I've lived my life for others. Always concerned with other's thoughts and opinions. Although I've tried not to show it, I always cared how others viewed me."

"I think that's human nature. We all care to some extent," Valen replied lighting another cigarette – a new habit he had started.

"Yes, but my aunt died never truly knowing me. It's made me a hard man, Valen. So, now, here, I want to tell you something," Samuel's voice shook from the anxiety inside him.

"What? Have you killed someone?" Valen asked with staged anticipation.

"No.... I've done a lot of crazy stuff, but haven't killed anyone – at least not yet. But I have had some adventurous livin'. Got some crazy tattoos in some crazy places, and along the way, I guess I got a little too careless and well, the truth is...I have HIV."

"What?" Valen dropped his cigarette into his lap, and leaped frantically to keep it from burning his leg.

Valen couldn't respond. He didn't know how. Valen squirmed nervously in his seat. All of a sudden everything had changed.

Samuel noticed the discomfort in Valen's eyes. "I didn't want to make you nervous, but I felt as though I had to tell you. We've roomed together for several months now, and I wanted you to know."

"I'm glad you told me," Valen smiled, but wasn't quite sure how to respond.

Sam laughed at Valen's squirming and poured another drink. "HIV impacts the lives of many people, and I am one of them. It doesn't mean you're going to catch it just by sitting here with me."

Valen sighed a silent breath of embarrassment, but still felt uncomfortable with the situation.

"Knowing I have this can lead me into deep isolation and

depression at times. I haven't ever shared this, and I was nervous to do so with you. None of it makes sense to me and I have been through every emotion possible. I've even asked God why He allowed this to happen to me and perhaps I have even turned my back on Him. After all, if He's supposed to be a God of love, why does He allow all this sickness, hunger and pain to continue? Why doesn't He just stop it, if He's so powerful?

Valen stammered in thought. He didn't know the Bible as well as he knew he should, but he did know God wasn't the cause of every struggle. Sherman had taught him that much.

"I don't know all the answers Sam," Valen sighed. "And I have faced plenty of hardships in my own life, but I did have a friend, who endured more pain and suffering I can't even fathom through a violent and tragic loss of his family. He too asked those same questions of God, but instead of turning away, He turned toward Him. As a result, his tragedy was used to bring hope and healing to many. He was a powerful man, but not by what he had, but because of his faith. Admittedly, I don't have his level of faith. For I know I am still chasing something I have yet to find, but his memory and testimony still penetrate my heart and mind. I wish you could have met him. I bet he would know what to say to you. For sadly, I do not.

As a result, Valen avoided the "Jesus" discussion. He hadn't sought the answers to his own questions and in many ways was being torn by two worlds, drifting deeper towards the desires of his flesh. So, instead, he simply apologized. "I hope you forgive my earlier shock. It's just that you kind of threw me off guard. After all, you did kinda' spring it on me."

"Yes, and it feels good to have someone know. Thanks for

listening." Sam threw back the last sip of beer and looked around the room of hardened men. "Besides, I don't see anyone else in this room I could talk to," he said winking. He stood, putting out his cigarette, "Let's go."

Valen was still uneasy, and felt guilty for not sharing more of his faith. He didn't know why he held back, but as he also looked around the room, he couldn't help but think how everyone there seemed to be missing the one truth he had. So, why was he unwilling to share? He wished he was more bold.

The two walked the beach for several miles back to the house, neither said a word, they just walked together with their thoughts.

Chapter VIII

Time passed, and Rhiannon's career kept growing. She remained true to her profession, despite her uneasiness. However, she honestly didn't know what else to do. She was a dramatic, powerful and successful attorney and was afraid - afraid to fail. She knew a lot of her friends had quit law and went into other avenues. Some opened businesses, others became writers and some even teachers, but Rhiannon couldn't. She was a rising star at the firm, and so, that's where she stayed.

With each morning, it was getting harder and harder to get up. Her job wasn't as much fun as it used to be. Many times, she'd hit the snooze button on her alarm at least four times, and take extra-long showers; but when she walked through the office doors, her poker face was on, and she was all charm. No one would ever guess that she was unhappy, but then again, that's what helped make her good at her job.

Her most recent promotion in the firm required a lot of travel abroad. She would meet with foreign businesses to go over claims and lawsuits. She enjoyed it because she got to experience so many different cultures, people and cuisines. Every city, every state and every country held something unique for her. She did enjoy that part of her job. However, she was seeing these places alone and longed for someone to share them with.

She wanted to feel as carefree and happy as she did when she was younger and with Valen.

One night, Rhiannon raced home and immediately snuggled into her favorite pajamas. She took the phone off the hook, put in a jazz CD and made herself some hot tea. She needed some time to get her thoughts together. Her mind felt so clouded. She was still in love with a man she may never see again, which she knew was ridiculous. But tonight she wanted to remember.

All the lights were out and a single candle burned. The mood was perfect. She sipped her tea and all the troubles she had were slowly washing away. The music created a journey, which her mind traveled. She remembered and saw places and faces she loved. Soon, she was asleep.

The next morning, Rhiannon found herself still on the couch. Her mind was fresh and clean, clouded only with last night's dreams. She had been racing around so much that she couldn't remember the last time she took a break for herself. She went to work with renewed hopes.

Days continued to pass, and soon, the rat race began to pick back up. Rhiannon looked forward to her next scheduled trip abroad. This time, it was to be London.

One of her client's there was having legal difficulties, and her services were going to be needed for a while. So, she got things together at home and booked a small one- bedroom apartment in London. She could hardly wait. She loved London and was hoping to make a fresh start there. She was getting older and knew she had to quit with her childish fantasies and thoughts of Valen. She needed to go on with her life, completely. Perhaps she could do it there.

Chapter IX

While working as a dock man, Valen spent much of his time writing and taking photos. His collection was becoming diverse, and he was finding joy in what he did. Valen's pictures included the beautiful landscape that surrounded him, the townspeople and even some animals caught in humorous situations. Valen eventually began incorporating his photographs with his writing to make homemade greeting cards. He and Sam would sell them on the weekends outside the local market and inside the bars. Surprisingly, he was making enough to even start saving a little. In fact, his cards quickly became a local sensation and the pride of the town. The locals enjoyed seeing their city displayed in such a beautiful fashion, and the words Valen wrote were catchy and edgy. He had cards for every occasion - missing you, the holidays, thank-you and so on.

Samuel would often laugh at Valen's excitement. His joy was overwhelming and contagious. Valen had finally found his niche, and Sam would often volunteer to help develop the photographs, which allowed Valen more time to sell and make cards.

The business was really taking off. Just after a year, Valen was able to quit his job at the loading docks and pursue his business full time. He was generating a pretty decent income too. Word of his unique, heart-felt cards filtered into other cities, and people soon began requesting his cards from state-to-state. To meet the demand, Valen published a catalog displaying all of his works. Valen was now gaining national praise. He was written about in several magazines and newspapers as an overnight success. Valen built the old shack where he and Samuel lived into his office and hired Samuel to be vice-president of the new company, Imaginations.

Sam and Valen tried to keep up with the demands. People simply couldn't get enough of the cards. Many were amazed with the emotion captured in the photographs, while others sought the cards for the poetry that expressed their emotions so well. Either way, people hungered for the art created in that beach shack.

It wasn't long before the word of Imaginations spread to the corporate offices of a major publisher. They were curious as to what all the excitement was about. So, they sent some representatives down to the island to check out Valen and his new company.

The two men they sent arrived in black, three-piece suits and both carried a briefcase. They had phones hanging from the right side of their belts and phones hanging from the left. They resembled FBI agents in appearance and stuck out like sore thumbs when they drove into town.

Valen and Samuel were in the local tavern working on some prose to accompany the next batch of photos.

Unfamiliar with their new surroundings, the two men began asking some of the locals if they knew of a Valen McCloud and where they could find him. They were immediately pointed to the bar.

Valen had just lit his last cigarette when the silhouette of two men cast a shadow before him. Valen turned and nudged Samuel as he pointed toward the door.

Both men looked around the bar as if they knew who they were looking for. However, it was a fairly rough crowd attending the bar that evening and the men soon gave up. Instead, they decided to approach the bartender.

"Excuse me," the tallest man said. He had jet black hair and wore thin metal-framed glasses. "Could you tell me if a Valen McCloud is here?"

The bar tender pointed to the far corner of the room.

As the men walked across the bar, snickering could be heard from all around. All these hard seamen couldn't believe how starched these two guys were.

When the men finally made their way through the tables and chairs, they helped themselves to a seat, between Samuel and Valen.

Without saying a word, they smiled and stared directly at Valen. Their discouragement to his appearance was apparent. They immediately thought he was too young to be the Valen McCloud they were looking for. So, they turned their attention to Samuel.

"Excuse me sir, but are you Mr. Valen McCloud?"

Samuel chuckled in amusement. "I hope not!" Sam smiled, putting his hand on Valen's shoulder. "This is your guy."

In an attempt to cover their shame, the two men stood up, and quickly extended their hand. "It's a pleasure to meet you, sir. We've been hearing a lot about you."

"That so?" Valen said rising to meet their handshake.

"Yes sir! My name is John Ricks, and this is my associate, Scott

Mills," he smiled gesturing to the small balding man on his right. Scott said very little. He just seemed to smile a lot.

"I see," Valen grinned. "Well it's a pleasure to meet you both." Valen was excited, but suspicious at the same time. "This is my partner, Samuel Travers," he said slapping Sam on the back.

Sam remained seated, "Nice to meet you, both," he said gesturing for everyone to sit back down. "To what do we owe the pleasure?" he asked.

"Well," John said, "We were hoping to get to know you and your business, a little better."

"Why?" Valen immediately asked.

"Well, to be quite frank with you sir, our publishing firm may be interested in buying your little company."

"Is that so," Valen smiled.

"Yes sir, and if we like what we see, we're willing to pay you a handsome profit," John smiled patting his briefcase.

Samuel's eyebrow rose a bit, as he reached into his shirt pocket for his lighter. Valen just sat there quietly and listened.

"We were hoping that maybe you could take us to your office so that we may get to know you and your business a little better," John said confidently.

"Sure," Valen said calmly. He was still a bit suspicious of the two men. If there was one thing he learned since he'd been out on his own was that trust was something to be earned.

Valen and Sam walked the two men down towards the beach. The men looked stiff and rigid as they tried to keep their shoes from getting too dirty. Valen glanced at Samuel and just laughed.

"How much farther?" John asked.

"Not much," Sam replied. "It's just past that bend," he said pointing past the dunes.

As the men approached the office of Imaginations, they gasped, and looked at one another. "Is this it?" John asked.

"This is it." Valen said coyly.

John looked at his partner in dismay. It was apparent they didn't understand how such a respected business was coming out of a rundown shack and being run by two bar flies. Yet still, they were sent for a reason and had a job to do.

"Well, let me take you on the nickel tour," Sam said, as he gestured his hand across the room. "This is where we develop the photos," he said pointing to the bathroom. "And this is where we come up with phrases and poems," he smiled pointing to the kitchen table. "The cards are put together and the catalogue is printed right here," he said patting their newly purchased computer.

The two men couldn't believe what they were seeing, but being the trained salesmen they were, they quickly played into their roles.

"Wonderful! It's amazing how you guys made Imaginations so successful. You must be proud," John said gracefully.

"Yes, we are," Valen replied. "But mostly we do what we do for self-expression and for fun."

"Excellent!" John smiled. "Well, what do you say we get down to business."

John gestured for everyone to sit down around the kitchen table, as he placed his briefcase down. "Our firm has been extremely impressed with the response your cards have been receiving. In fact, we've seen a decline in sales for our product here on the island since Imaginations was started. Anyway, to be frank, we would like to make you an offer for the company. What would you say a fair offer to be?"

"I have no idea," Valen shrugged.

"Well, what was your total revenue last year and how are you looking year-to-date?"

"Last year we broke a million, and this year we're likely to at least double that," Valen stated confidently.

The two men shared glances and continued. "We feel Imaginations would be a strong complement to our family of greeting cards," John opened the briefcase. "We would like to keep you on as consultants of course, after all, this is your vision and talent at work. However, overtime you may feel comfortable with our abilities to keep the integrity of your work true, and at that time, you may decide to retire from the business altogether. Anyway, with all that being said, we feel a fair price based on your current production and projected revenue is this." John pulled a check from his briefcase and slid it face down over to Valen. "Please, pick it up and look at it, I believe you'll find it more that generous," John stated most sincerely.

"This has got to be a joke!" Valen gasped as he looked at the offer.

"It's no joke, sir," the short quiet guy said sternly. "Plus royalties on all your original works."

Samuel just sat there without expression. "You'll have to excuse me while I confer with my associate," Valen said pulling at Sam's shirt.

"Three million dollars! Can you believe it, Sam?" Valen whispered with great excitement. "What do you think?"

"I don't know what to think, Valen. It seems like a good deal to me, but the real question is what do you think?"

"I like it Sam. I can take pictures and write prose all I want. Now, I can decide to do it and be rich at the same time."

"Sounds like you made up your mind. So, go for it." Samuel said calmly.

"Yeah! I think I will," Valen approached the two men, now admiring the beach. "Guys, you have yourselves a deal. So, what's next?"

"Nothing, all you have to do is sign these papers, and cash the check," John said handing him a vanilla envelope. "Of course, you will be expected to hand over all rights and property of Imaginations...the house, computer, everything. And there is a no compete clause, meaning you can't open another greeting card business. However, as I stated earlier, we need you to stay on as a consultant for at least one year. We need to train our staff to your form. You may consult via email, teleconference, or in person, that is up to you."

"I see," Valen thought. "Sam is included as a consultant, correct?"

"That is up to you, sir. He will be on your payroll, though, not ours."

Valen looked at Sam. "I'm fine with whatever you decide," Sam smiled.

"Okay, you have yourself a deal," Valen gleamed. "Now, show me where to sign...I will get a copy of these documents?" he asked.

"Of course!" John replied.

"Well," Valen extended his hand, "it was a pleasure doing business with you."

"For us, as well, sir," John smiled.

"Same for me, sir," Scott chimed in.

Valen glanced over to see if Samuel was there, but he was nowhere to be seen.

"Well, I'm sure I speak for Samuel, when I say, thank you. Can you stay for dinner?"

"No thanks, we appreciate the offer, but we really must head back to the office. There's a lot to get done," John said as he stuffed the signed papers in his briefcase. "But first, let's get you some copies made."

"Here," Valen gestured back toward the house, "you can do it in there."

After all the papers were copied and the two men were gone, Valen sat back and reflected on what just happened. "I'm rich," he said aloud, "By God, I did it." He said proudly. Never once acknowledging God, other than simply stating His name.

His excitement overcame him and he jumped up to look for Sam. They had some celebrating to do, but again, Sam was nowhere to be found.

"Now where would he go?" He thought aloud.

Valen walked to the bar first, but Sam wasn't there. He tried the docks, but Samuel wasn't there either, when suddenly, it dawned on him...the lighthouse.

Sam always went to the lighthouse just over the dunes when he wanted to be alone. It was his sanctuary, and his place of thought.

Out of breath, Valen smiled. "I thought I'd find you here," he said cheerfully.

"Good work detective," Samuel said sarcastically.

"So, what made you decide to come all the way out here? Aren't you happy? I mean, we're millionaires!" Valen cheered.

"Valen, let's get something straight. You are the millionaire. The business was yours and you're the one that sold it. Imaginations was the one thing I was ever proud of. To me, it had no price tag."

"Sam, what are you talking about? You said we should sell."

"No, I told you to do whatever you wanted. Listen, I don't expect you to understand. You're young and you're a dreamer, but for me, Imaginations gave my life some extra validation, some purpose. Now it's gone."

"Samuel, you're totally missing the point. I understand what you're saying, but you can always create greeting cards, we just can't sell them. The fun part was creating them anyway. We just got lucky that people ended up wanting to buy so many of them. So, nothing's gone, we've simply taken another step. There are many cookie jars in this world, and I want to have my hand in a lot of them, not just one. Imaginations satisfied one hunger, but now I want something different. Sam, can't you see, you can always create, just because Imaginations was sold doesn't mean you can't still continue your passion. I just have others that need to be satisfied," Valen smiled.

"I know all that! I just enjoyed our team. We made a good team! Listen - I sound like a foolish child, never mind, just never mind," Sam sighed.

Valen sat quietly. It was funny, but ever since he and Rhiannon had gone their separate ways, his emotions for others seemed to have dulled. He, ironically, felt no remorse or sorrow for his friend, Sam. He simply didn't care, or perhaps he didn't want to care.

"Sam, calm down. I understand what you're saying. We're still a team...always will be. Be happy in the fact that you found a passion, some people never find, or even pursue one, and on top of that, you're rich. You can do whatever you want. Try to think about the new opportunities you have now."

Sam sighed, "I know. I know, you're right, but you need to stop saying we are rich. It's you who's rich," he smiled.

Valen put his arm around Sam. "It's okay. Now com'on. What do ya' say we go get something to drink and celebrate?"

"Sounds good," Sam said as he stood, brushing himself off, "let's go."

Chapter X

Rhiannon had found a great apartment in London and was beginning to feel right at home. Her client was a joy to work for and before long they became good friends.

His name was Byron Parnel, a wealthy English gentleman, who had inherited most of his money. His grandfather was the second largest distributor of raw steel in England, and the family was one of the top clients at Rhiannon's firm. So, being that Byron was having tax issues, the firm's rising star, Rhiannon, was sent to get things back in order.

Byron and Rhiannon spent many nights going over his past expense records. Thus, having plenty of time to get to know one another. Byron was more than twice Rhiannon's age so naturally Rhiannon saw nothing between them, but friendship. However, Byron had other ideas.

He would take Rhiannon to fancy restaurants, and they made frequent appearances to the ballet, opera and theater. Byron was a lover of the arts, as well as beautiful artifacts. Unfortunately, his love was more for the statement and impression art made and not for the appreciation of it.

When not with Byron, Rhiannon spent much of her time in town. She had grown to love the simplistic hustle of European life. She felt safe there. However, her thoughts still drifted to Valen. To help reflect her memories, Rhiannon took up photography. Not only did it help bring her closer to Valen, but she found that she was quite good. She had the rare talent of being able to capture specific moments in people's lives without being too invasive. Also, people liked her. They would reveal themselves to her, and she did not pass judgment.

Rhiannon's peace was soon distracted when she began to uncover discrepancies in Byron's taxes. Eventually, she discovered Byron was involved in illegal activities and was filtering money through real estate, investment houses and even her law firm. In fact, Rhiannon was one of the puppets being naively used to help filter some of this money clean.

She decided not to say a word to her company yet, until she had concrete evidence, or to Byron, for the fear of not knowing what he would do if he suspected she knew anything. So, they continued with their cordial congenialities, and Rhiannon hid behind the smiling persona she had perfected so well.

Chapter XI

It was about sunrise when Valen and Sam finally returned home from celebrating. They had talked all night, but Valen's mind was now racing with ideas of what he could do next. He was definitely curious about tracking down Rhiannon. He wanted to be with her, but how? So many years had passed since they went their separate ways.

Ironically, they had set out to chase down the dreams they so passionately embraced when they were younger. However, now that they accomplished them, they found they were both left with an emptiness no amount of money, success or promotion could satisfy.

As a result, Valen began to question what his pursuits had truly gotten him. He was rich, something he always wanted, but the happiness he thought would come from it never did. Just a short burst, and then it was gone. His restlessness was creeping back. For now, he could go practically anywhere he wanted, buy what he wanted and do pretty much what he wanted, but he realized he had no one to share it with. At a time when many would radiate happiness, my father was still searching for more.

As the sun's glow reflected off the ocean, Valen's eyes filled with tears. His thoughts focused on finding Rhiannon. That was his new mission. Perhaps she could once again fill his heart and life with the love they once knew. The ocean water cascaded around his angles and pulled sand out from under his feet. He smiled in anticipation of the days ahead as he watched his feet sink deeper and deeper into the sand.

Valen wondered if she still loved him. She could have met someone by now, he thought. Would she be happy to see him, or would she be bothered? Perhaps she would dread to see him? He was ready to know her response so that he could go on with his life either way - with or without her. Immediately, he thought of Rhiannon's mother. He still had their old home number, and perhaps, she could shed some light on the best way to find Rhiannon.

"Hello?" A soft voice answered.

Valen was nervous at first and hesitated.

"Hello?" The voice answered again.

"Uh...hello? May I speak to Mrs. Elizabeth?"

"This is Liz."

"Hi, m'am, this is Valen."

"Valen! How good to hear from you! How are you?" she shouted as if never remembering kicking him off her property.

"Good. I hope everything is going well there." Valen stammered.

"Well, as good as can be expected I suppose."

"How's your son, Christopher?"

"He's fine, happy as ever. He's out back climbing our oak trees now," she laughed

Valen laughed hesitantly and was silent for a while, "Mrs. Elizabeth...," he began.

"Call me Liz, Valen. It's okay."

"Yes'm. Uhm...Liz, I'm going to get right to the point. I'm looking for Rhiannon and was hoping that you could help me find her."

"Really? I think that's great! You know, I don't think she has ever gotten over you Valen. You made quite an impression on us all," she said in full southern charm.

"Well, I appreciate that m'am. I haven't been able to get her out of my mind. She made quite an impression on me I can assure you. So, you will help me find her?"

"I'd be more than happy to, but I think it's going to be difficult for you to get to her. She's in London."

"London?"

"Yes. She has a job there. She's a lawyer you know?"

"No, I knew that's what she wanted to do, but I had no idea she actually did it, but then again, I'm not surprised. Rhiannon was always determined." Valen's mind reflected back to the day they parted ways.

"That's true," Elizabeth responded. "She's always been full of fire and independence. I'd like to say she got it from me, but in truth, her father gets all the credit."

"Yes, I heard a lot of good things about him."

"He was a good man, Valen, and I think he would've liked you. In fact, you always kind of remind me of him.

"Wish I could've known him," Valen's response ended in a

107

comfortable silence. He could sense Liz's loneliness and love for her past husband. The both of them sat with the phone to their ears, not saying a word.

Finally, Liz broke the silence, "I hope you find her, Valen. I know she would like to see you again."

"I will Mrs. Elizabeth. I have to."

"Hold on and let me get her phone number for you...Are you ready?"

"Yes m'am."

Valen excitedly wrote down the number. "Okay, I got it. I appreciate your help."

"It's no problem. Good luck, Valen. I hope to see you again soon. And I know it was a long time ago, but I want to apologize for overreacting the last time we saw each other."

"It's fine. I understand. If it was my daughter being brought back at six in the morning, I would've been mad too."

Valen hung up the phone comforted with fond memories. He drifted back to his first encounters with Rhiannon and reflected on how nervous he was when he first arrived at her house. He remembered his hunger for wealth and his initial intimidation to Rhiannon's mother and her money. Now, they spoke like old buddies, and he had accomplished his dream for wealth. He thought it interesting how time unfolds. He found it ironic how his thirst for money was quenched in an unexpected way. It was his passion for writing and photography that granted him his newfound wealth. At an earlier time, Valen would have bet money could never be earned by something as seemingly frivolous as pictures and prose. Following his heart had paid off in the material world. Now, he just hoped it would work for him in love's world as well.

The next day, Valen raced to the nearest jewelry store to find Rhiannon the perfect ring. If he was going to find her, he was going to go all in. At first, he thought of designing the ring with elegant engravings, but the more he looked and the more he thought of Rhiannon's personality, he knew that simple was the way to go. The first ring that caught his eye was a full carat that was practically flawless. It was held by five prongs and sat on a simple gold band. It was simple, stated its purpose and was classic. It was perfect.

That night, Valen held the ring up to the moon and marveled at its sparkle. The beauty competed with the stars'. He thought of how it would look on Rhiannon's finger and tried to imagine her reaction. He couldn't wait.

Highways End

Chapter XII

Rhiannon continued to do her job as expected, not hinting any knowledge of Byron's misgivings. However, when they would go out, she couldn't help but look at him differently. She was disgusted that this suave, kind and generous man was behind this sort of corruption. She naively thought the stereotypical shifty-eyed fast talker would be involved in such activities, but Byron, by all appearances, was a perfect gentleman.

One night, during one of their shared dinners, Byron's actions began to make her nervous. He was behaving peculiar and was overly inquisitive. "I've noticed you're not your cheerful self lately my dear, and I was wondering what was troubling you?" Byron's lips curled in a suspicious grin.

Rhiannon uncomfortable with the question, began playing with her food.

"Nothing," she said, upon realizing her behavior and trying to act normal.

"Really?" he smiled. "Are you sure? Because if anything's troubling you, I'd like to know. It's important to me that you're comfortable. I mean after-all,' Byron laughed, 'I don't want our best attorney unsettled." Byron's smile dropped into a solemn expression, "I'm sure you understand."

Rhiannon understood perfectly what he was saying. Somehow her suspicions and feelings had been read and Byron, being very on guard, was quick to notice her slight change in personality.

111

"Sure I understand," Rhiannon said nonchalantly, "Why do you ask?"

Confident that he made his point clear, Byron changed the subject. "No reason," Byron said calmly. "So, how are those pictures of yours turning out?"

The rest of the night was a tortuous charade of small talk. When the night was over, Rhiannon found herself locking her doors and shaking profusely.

"I can't believe what I've gotten' myself into," she thought. "I can't continue doing this," her mind raced. "I've got to get out of this situation and fast, but how?"

Chapter XIII

Valen told Samuel about his idea of trying to find Rhiannon. Samuel, being confused by the abrupt decision stammered for words. "When did...How...What?"

Valen smiled. "I know it's sudden, but this part of my life is done now, and it's time to start the other. I'm going to miss you, Sam," Valen placed his hand on Sam's shoulder. "You and I are forever friends, but it's time for me to go after what I need. And I need her. She's my happiness, always has been."

Samuel smiled at the thought. "I know, my friend. Good luck, and keep me posted," he said grabbing Valen for a hug. "Thank you for all you've done."

"Sam," Valen smiled, "we've helped each other and had a good time doing it. Thank you."

Samuel smiled. "What about your contract with the card company. Don't you have to stay on a year?"

"Well, I was hoping that's where you would help me. You'll be on my payroll of course," Valen smiled hoping Sam would agree to stay.

"Of course – It would be my privilege, but they may request you from time-to-time. What would you like me to do?"

Valen turned and began to walk away. "I'll be in touch," he shouted. "And will send pictures - don't worry!"

At the airport, Valen purchased a first class ticket to London and could hardly wait for the plane to take off. He tried to settle his nerves and instead of prayer, he decided to slow his mind with a couple glasses of wine. After his first drink, he sat back and prepared for take-off. He always enjoyed the sensation of lift-off and the drop it left in his stomach.

In the air, Valen ordered one more glass and removed the journal from his backpack stuffed under the seat in front of him. He laughed at how beaten up it looked. The leather was scratched and faded, and the binding was falling apart. Stuffed between the pages were various napkins from cafes he had scribbled his thoughts on over the years. All was held together by two large rubber bands. Valen searched for a blank page and began to relieve his brain of all the fear and excitement he was experiencing from the idea of seeing Rhiannon again. He wrote for most of the flight, and by the time the plane landed in London, he was drained and exhausted.

Outside the airport, he hailed a cab to take him to the nearest and cleanest hotel in the area. Within minutes, Valen was checked in his room and dove into his undisturbed bed, fully dressed.

The next morning, Valen began the duty of unpacking his luggage. After a long shower, he dressed and was in the lobby by noon. Hungry, he decided to grab a quick lunch in the hotel's deli.

"Sorry, sir," the waitress said politely, "but you'll need to exchange this at the front counter."

Realizing he hadn't exchanged his money, Valen apologized and was quick to return with the appropriate currency. As he ate his sandwich, the reality of where he was and what he was doing began to dawn on him.

"What am I doing?' he thought. "How do I expect to find her here?" "I must be crazy," he said aloud as he laughed at himself with a mouthful of bread.

Upon finishing his meal, Valen slung his camera around his neck and set out on the streets of London to familiarize himself with his surroundings. "How Charles Dickens'ish," he thought. Valen was more on the outskirts of the city where the smell of hundreds year old wood filled the air. He was awed and comforted by the old buildings. They inspired a sense of warmth and were beautiful in their simplistic, yet intricate designs. The old cabs were a treasure, and the whole city itself seemed to muster up a nostalgic past.

After a few hours of site seeing, Valen decided he had wasted enough time and walked to the nearest phone booth. It was bright red and quite different from the booths he was used to in the states. He took a few breaths, dialed the number and as the phone rang, he found himself shivering as if cold. His nerves were completely on wire and alert. His palms were sweating, and he could feel his heart in his stomach. The phone continued to ring. There was no answer, and in a way, he was relieved. "I'll try again later," he thought, and he walked further into the city.

Valen made his way to the subway, or underground and took a ride. He had never been to London before, but managed to make his way around like a native. It was in his rambling soul to be comfortable on the road, and he wasn't afraid to wander off, or to get lost. He trusted he could always find his way back.

Valen rode the rail all the way to a place called Covent Garden. It was a tourist stop, but was filled with the most wonderful little shops, similar to a flea market. Booths were set up for the various merchants and craftsmen to sell their costume jewelry, woodcarvings, clothes, tools and even home-cooked meals. The market's streets were swarmed with people. People were singing, dancing and entertaining with magic acts. The fresh scent of baked breads filled the air and almost everyone was wearing a smile that day. Valen loved it! He set his camera and began shooting rolls of film. Life was everywhere, and he wanted to capture it all.

After several hours of sightseeing, Valen's stomach began to ache with hunger. So, he decided to delight his taste buds with some of the side-street cuisines that filled the air with its delicious aroma. His first order was for a sausage dog and loaded baked potato, both being the largest he had ever seen. The potato in particular was enormous, yet so soft it was like slicing butter; and the sausage was delectably greasy. Valen savored every bite.

When finished, his pants felt as if they were about to pop open, but he felt good. The sun was shining on his face, children were laughing in the park and his stomach was full. The only thing he needed now was Rhiannon, and his intuition told him that the time was soon.

Valen made his way back to the center of the market and began browsing all the merchandise. He was impressed at how wonderfully crafted many of the items were. What caught his eye in particular was a rope necklace with a cross. It was sculpted from some black, metallic looking stone. Valen thought it was beautiful in every detail, and in some way, it soothed him. Without a haggle, Valen immediately purchased the cross and tied it around his neck. It was then, with renewed confidence he decided to call Rhiannon.

Again, he walked to the nearest phone and began dialing her number, but this time, a peculiar feeling came over him. He hung up immediately. Among all the scents in the air, he noticed a faint sweetness he hadn't smelled in years. It was familiar, yet new. Suddenly, as Valen turned to walk the other direction, he was nearly run over by a woman on a bike.

"Sorry!" the woman shouted barely turning to notice if he was okay.

Brushing himself off, Valen caught a quick glance of the woman. It was Rhiannon! Or at least it looked like her, and the scent of her perfume still hung in the air. Valen remembered it to be the same she once wore.

"Hey! Wait!" he shouted, but the woman was half way down the court.

The similarities were too coincidental, and without thought, Valen began running after her. Desperate, he quickly stopped a small boy riding on his bike.

"Hey, kid. I'll give you...' Valen grabbed all the money from his pockets, and quickly counted it, 'all this for your bike'."

The boy looked at Valen as if he were mad.

"Please!" Valen begged desperately, pushing the money in the boy's hands.

"Sure," the boy said joyfully, as he shoved the money in his pockets.

Valen immediately jumped on his new purchase and began

peddling madly. The bike was too small for Valen's size, but he managed the best he could. All the onlookers however, couldn't help but laugh. Valen could barely see Rhiannon in the distance. He would have to hurry if he wanted to catch her. Faster and faster he peddled until his legs burned from exhaustion, yet he kept on. He was getting closer, and he had but one focus - to catch her. It was as if all the years past were suddenly compacted into this one moment. All his memories, all his desires and all his love was forcing him to go faster.

"Rhiannon!" he shouted, "Rhiannon!" But she could not hear him. Valen leaned forward in an attempt to get closer, "Rhiannon! Please stop, it's Valen! Sto...," but before he could complete his sentence he stumbled over a rock and went skidding over the pavement and into the grass. He wasn't hurt, but he just laid there in tired frustration. Some people began gathering around asking if he was okay, but being frustrated he just shunned them off with his hand.

"Yes, yes," he said. "Please, I'd just like to lay here. Thanks for your concern."

Then one of the voices stood out. "Valen?" It sounded like an angel. "Valen, is that you?" On reflex, Valen leaned up.

"Rhiannon?" he asked looking around.

"Valen!" she shouted, jumping towards him and knocking him back to the ground. "I don't believe it! It's you," she cried rubbing his face and hair. "Are you okay?"

"Yes," he said smiling, "I'm fine." They grabbed each other in huge hugs.

Soon the crowd dispersed, and Valen and Rhiannon were left alone, alone for the first time in several years. It was a bittersweet reunion, but they were both happy to be together again.

"How've you been?" Valen asked. He interrupted before she could answer. "You're so beautiful, Rhian," he said waving his hand through her soft hair. "You haven't changed a bit." Rhiannon was silenced by his words. She hadn't been touched that gently, or spoken to that sincerely in a long time.

"I've missed you," she whispered.

"Oh, I've missed you too. I haven't been able to get you out of my mind. My heart feels as if we never parted," Valen responded.

"I know the feeling," Rhiannon said running her finger down the bridge of his nose.

Neither lifted themselves off the ground. They just sat there and enjoyed each other's company. Several minutes had past when they both decided to take a walk. Valen lifted his miniature bike and began walking along side Rhiannon. "Where did you get that bike," Rhiannon said laughing at its size.

"What, you don't like my bike?" Valen smiled. "This is the newest thing. I like your bike, by the way. It's quite fast."

"Yes, just trying to catch some exercise. This is a great place to take a ride," she smiled.

Just then, Valen saw a little girl playing by a puddle, and he walked up to her.

"Hi there," he said. "I was wondering, do you know who would like to have this bike? As you can see I've out grown it, but I don't want to throw it away." The little girl was shy, but was excited about the opportunity presented to her.

"I'll take care of it," she said softly.

"I sure would appreciate it if you would. Do you know how to ride it?" Valen asked.

The little girl nodded excitedly, jumped on the bike and began to ride.

"Sure do," she said waving as she rode away. Valen and Rhiannon both laughed.

"Still winning the little girls' hearts I see," Rhiannon said wrapping her arm around Valen's neck.

"I sure hope so," Valen smiled.

Rhiannon parked her bike against a nearby tree, and they continued their walk until dusk talking about old times. Neither seemed to acknowledge the fact that several years had past since they'd last seen each other. They simply didn't care. "Where are you staying?" Rhiannon asked.

"I'm not sure of the hotels name, but I think I know how to get back there," Valen smiled.

"How 'bout you? Do you live far from here?"

"No, I'm actually right around the corner."

When they arrived at Rhiannon's door, Valen began to fidget like a schoolboy. He awkwardly took her hand. "Rhiannon?" he asked. "If possible, I was hoping that I could take you out to dinner...or something, tomorrow?"

Rhiannon smiled at his sincerity and was struck by his weathered good looks. He had aged well since she last seen him. "Sure," she said. "Does seven o'clock sound okay?"

"Absolutely!" Valen replied, as he kissed her on the cheek.

Walking backwards to leave, Valen smiled and waved, "I'll see you at seven, Rhiannon."

Rhiannon stood on her doorstep and waved good-bye. She couldn't believe it was really him.

Valen walked that night with a permanent smile on his face. He wasn't ready to go back to the quietness of his hotel. So, he stopped at one of the pubs he saw on the corner. It appeared to be very old and was decorated with an extreme number of overflowing plants. So, Valen thought it would be an interesting one to check out.

Upon entering the pub, Valen noticed it was a quiet night. Only two men sat at the bar. "I'll have a Guinness," Valen directed politely.

"Right away," the man behind the bar said without emotion.

Valen sat and thought of the evening he had with Rhiannon. It was incredible how he came across her. He knew it was all meant to be. However, despite having his newly purchased cross hanging around his neck, he still neglected to make any effort in seeking the One the cross represented.

"Your pint, sir," the bartender smiled. "You're not from the colonies are you?" He said sarcastically.

"I'm sorry?" Valen asked.

"You know, the colonies," the man smiled. "the states?"

"Oh," Valen laughed. "I've never heard America described that way. Yes, as a matter of fact I am. Is it that obvious?" Valen smiled.

"Yes," the man responded.

Valen was comforted by the man's warm nature. He was a plump, jolly looking fellow, with rosy cheeks. He was nearing his seventies, and Valen could tell he spent most of his time napping away the day and working the nights.

"I always wanted to go to America, but never quite got the opportunity. This pub can't run itself."

"No, I guess not," Valen responded. "Is this your place?"

"Yes, my father left it to me, and his father left it to him."

"It's nice," Valen smiled looking around. "It's very comfortable here.

"Thank you. I like it, but again, I would really like the chance to visit America someday."

"Yes, you should try," Valen agreed. "I think you'd enjoy yourself. Where would you most like to visit?"

"Well, I have to see Disney World, of course, but then I think I'd like to see New York."

"Of course," Valen smiled. "I guess you kind of have to, but I'll tell ya', if you get the chance, try visiting some of the smaller towns. We have some very nice ones in the south where I'm from, like Charleston, South Carolina or Savannah, Georgia. I think you'd enjoy yourself."

"Really?" the man smiled. "I might do that. I have heard of those places."

"They're simple, yet beautiful. They also give you a flavor to the charm of what the old south used to be - like cobble stone roads and grand estate homes. But of course, they're only old in American standards. There's nothing quite like the buildings you have here."

Valen made a toasting gesture as he raised the last sip of his pint to his lips. "I think I'm ready for another."

"Right away, sir" the man nodded.

Chapter XIV

Seven o'clock the following evening came slow for both Valen and Rhiannon. Rhiannon could hardly concentrate on her work, and Valen felt as if he toured the entire city twice. Rhiannon had a meeting with Byron that day, and hoped he wouldn't ask her to go out that night. She simply didn't want to bother with making up some excuse.

During the meeting, Byron was his flirtatious and charming self. It made Rhiannon sick. She was getting bored with this "cat and mouse" routine.

"Rhiannon, my dear, you are doing a fantastic job. I just want you to know that," Byron said touching her hand. "I've contacted your boss and asked that he give you a bonus."

"Oh, Byron, you didn't have to do that, but I do appreciate it," Rhiannon said in a fake cheerful voice.

"Of course you do, dear. Now, let's say I treat you to an opera tonight. How's that sound?" Byron said confidently.

"It sounds fantastic, but I already have plans. I'm sorry Byron, perhaps another time. I do love the opera you know," Rhiannon replied.

"Yes, I know," Byron said jealously. "This must be some date."

Rhiannon was just about to deny her meeting with Valen, but then decided to be brutally honest. "Yes, yes it is," she smiled.

"I see. Well, have fun then," and with that, Byron stormed out of the room like a spoiled child. Rhiannon couldn't help but laugh inside. She couldn't wait until tonight. She had so many things to ask Valen.

During Rhiannon's meeting with Byron, Valen was mingling with all the locals on the street, taking their photos and learning English culture. He was surprised how London was a big city, and yet the police didn't carry guns. He also noticed how many of the pedestrians seemed to leave their bikes unlocked and unattended. It was something quite curious and new for him to witness. However, it quickly reminded him to go retrieve Rhiannon's bike which they had left leaning against a tree the night before. Again, to his surprise, it too was still there. "Impressive," he thought as he began riding it through town.

Of all the London treasures however, the pubs remained Valen's favorite. He enjoyed them mostly because good conversation could always be found there, and none were ever over-crowded. They were always filled with just enough people to get a universal discussion started. Valen felt relaxed in the dimly lit atmosphere and dark polished wood surroundings. And in almost every pub he entered, at least one autographed picture of at least one, or all of The Beatles could be found.

After a few hours of discussing world politics and soccer in a newer pub he recently discovered, Valen hurried back to the hotel, for a quick freshening-up. He made it to Rhiannon's door at precisely ten minutes before seven o'clock. As he knocked, the door slowly creaked open from not being shut completely.

"Hello? Rhiannon? Anyone here?"

"I'm upstairs," a faint voice echoed down the stairs. "Be down in a minute. Make yourself out home. There's some drinks in the fridge."

"Okay! Thanks."

Rhiannon's home was immaculate and was decorated in an old Victorian style, intermingled with a touch of southwest. Valen found it to be very comfortable and cozy. From the fridge, he pulled the only drink he could find. It was an apple juice fruit box and Valen laughed at the thought of why she would be keeping a fresh stock of those.

When Rhiannon stepped downstairs, it was like watching an angel descend upon earth. She was fantastically beautiful. Her hair glimmered with streaks of auburn, and her skin was gently tanned. Her lips, naturally pink. Rhiannon wore white sandals that strapped around her ankles, and a white summer dress.

Valen's heart pounded and his adrenaline rushed. The only words he could think to say were, "I found your bike."

"Perfect - thank you, Valen! I honestly forgot all about it - hope you enjoyed your day riding through town. London's quite beautiful don't you think?"

Valen didn't answer directly, instead he replied softly, "You look incredible." He could see Rhiannon blush slightly as she brushed her hair from her face.

"So, where should we go?" Valen asked getting himself back on focus. "What's good?"

"Well, I thought we could get some authentic English food. I know a great place just around the corner." Rhiannon smiled.

"Sounds good to me," Valen said as he opened the door gesturing for Rhiannon's lead.

"But is authentic English food supposed to be good?" He smiled.

It was a comfortable night, and Valen proposed that they walk. Like a schoolboy, all he could think of was holding her hand. He could feel her fingers brush softly against his hand as if hinting for him to take it. Then, casually, he touched the tips of her fingers and gradually wrapped his hand around hers. Her hand was soft and cool, and an old familiar shiver raced through his spine. Rhiannon felt like a flower, delicate and clean, and she provided him with a comfort that was lost for too long.

They stopped just a few blocks later at the cafe. It was dimly lit and an orange yellow glow filled the room. "You still like sparkling water?" Valen asked.

"I do," Rhiannon smiled playfully.

"Two sparkling waters please," Valen said waving to the barkeep.

"Right away, sir," the Englishman replied in his hard accent.

"So, tell me what you've been up to. We haven't spoken in how many years?"

"It's been too long," Rhiannon said as she reached across the table for Valen's hand.

"A lot has happened since we last saw each other, but I have to say, you haven't changed a bit, Valen. You're still as handsome as the first day I saw you."

"So are you, Rhiannon. Even more so - beautiful, I mean."

128

Valen's fingers brushed Rhiannon's hand softly. Memories raced through his mind and his heart ached with joy.

The old man returned a large frosted bottle of water and two glasses. "You two ready to order?" he asked as he brushed his hands dry from the drops of ice that had spilled.

The waiter was an older, bearded man that looked much like a pirate. His smile, although rarely exposed, was an honest one. He appeared to be a stern man, yet filled with a rare pride for his work. Valen liked him instantly.

"Yes sir," Valen nodded as he gestured toward Rhiannon to order.

"I'm going to have the shepherd's pie," she smiled.

"Fish and chips for me," Valen said.

"They're good," the old man said sharply as he walked away.

"I hope you like it, Val." Rhiannon smiled.

"How could I not – I'm with you," he winked.

Quickly, Valen changed the subject as he looked at Rhiannon intently. "Rhiannon. I have something to tell you."

"What is it? You look so serious."

"I don't mean to, but..," Valen hesitated and his mind wondered if he should tell her about his new found wealth so soon. Would she behave differently, or remain the same? He knew he was thinking too much about it and should just tell her, but something in him made him want to wait.

"But what?" Rhiannon urged.

"I talked to your mother before I left for England, and I was just wondering if she and Pete were still together," Valen was slightly ashamed at how well he could hide his true thoughts.

Rhiannon sighed, "Yea, unfortunately. He's just so nasty. He still gives me the creeps too. Honestly, every time I go home, I can feel his eyes looking me over. I don't know why she stays with him. She doesn't love him. She'll admit it, too. I just think she's lonely, and he provides company and can make her laugh."

"Maybe your right, but I never liked him either, and it's hard for me to see him with a sense of humor. He always seemed so serious to me."

"He is, but he's a professional kiss-up," Rhiannon smirked.

"Do you get home often?" Valen asked.

"Not really, I've been so busy after I got out of school, that the past few years have seemed to pass like days."

"I know the feeling."

"Now, enough about me. I'm dying to know what you've been doing," Rhiannon said as she tapped him with her foot under the table.

"Oh, not much really. I lived at the beach for a while."

"Really? What beach?"

"Off of the southern coast. It was beautiful down there. I really had a good time - lots of hard work, but a good time.

"What did you do and how long were you there?" Rhiannon leaned closer.

"I was there just a few years and mostly worked the docks, loading and unloading shipments. I also continued with my pictures and writing. Once you get outside of the docking zone, the rest of the countryside is truly beautiful."

"Valen, you crack me up. You've always done these different things - gone against the grain. You definitely live in your own little world.

"I know. It's fun here most of the time," Valen smiled innocently.

"Well, then what?" Rhiannon continued.

"What do you mean?"

"What did you do after the beach?"

"Oh, well like I said, I wrote quite a bit, but for the time before and after the beach, I was primarily on the road, just driving and enjoying the scenery. It helped clear my head as to what I wanted to do with my life."

"Were you on that old bike of yours?"

"Of course," Valen smiled nervously, knowing this conversation could easily head to what he did for a living.

"I can't believe that thing's still running. Where is it now?"

"I left it back with a friend."

"Who?"

"Sam. He's a friend I made while working on the fishing docks. He also helped me pursue my writing. He's a good guy."

"Valen, it seems like you've been busy."

"Yea, well I can tell I haven't been as busy as you. Look at ya'. You're an international lawyer living over here in England. You can't get much more impressive than that."

"Yes you can," she smiled softly.

"What do mean?"

"A family," Rhiannon said shyly.

Valen looked down and smiled.

"We're getting to that age you know," Rhiannon continued. "Some might still consider us young, but I think we're at that right time to start a family."

"I suppose you're right," Valen said, "but you have to make sure you're ready, you know?"

"I know. There aren't many good catches out there," Rhiannon said winking at Valen.

"Well, I never had to worry about that. I've always known who I wanted," Valen responded.

"Got your food here," the old man shouted as he served their plates.

"Looks good," Valen said.

When the waiter left, Valen looked at his watch and laughed. "Must take a little longer to get your food over here."

"Yea, things can move a little slower at times," Rhiannon smiled.

"I like it," Valen said cutting his fish.

"I do too."

When they finished, Valen personally thanked the old man for his service and asked him to recommend a romantic spot they could visit within walking distance. The man pointed them towards the river.

As Valen and Rhiannon walked, Rhiannon noticed the cross around Valen's neck. "I like it," she said holding it gently in the palm of her hand.

"Thanks, I found it when I got here. It just seemed to catch my eye." Valen untied it from his neck. "Here, I want you to have it."

"No, Valen please, I was just commenting on it. I didn't mean to insinuate I wanted it."

"I know. I want to give it to you. I was never given the chance before you left to give you anything, and I want you to have this. It would mean a lot to me," he said as he reached around her.

Rhiannon stood silent as he tied it around her neck. She had never received such a sincere gift, and she was touched. "Thank you, Valen," she said softly with tears in her eyes. "I'll treasure it always."

The cross represented something they both knew to be special, but yet, although they knew its truth they remained clouded to its greater meaning.

Standing under a lamp near the streets, Rhiannon seemed to radiate in the night. She was truly beautiful. Valen pulled her gently to him and kissed her. They never made it to the river.

Slowly, Rhiannon and Valen began walking back to her home. "Would you like to come in for a minute?" Rhiannon asked.

"I'd love to," he said without hesitation.

Valen walked in and followed Rhiannon to the couch.

"Here," she gestured for Valen to sit down, "make yourself comfortable, and I'll get you some warm tea."

"That would be great. Thank you."

Valen looked around the apartment at all the pictures Rhiannon had on display. He got up and walked over to the television. On top, sat several pictures of Rhiannon's college friends and office coworkers. On the coffee table, Valen found a photo album filled with pictures Rhiannon had obviously taken herself. They consisted of the areas and people she had met during her travels. Towards the back, Valen found an old picture of him sitting on his bike. He had no idea when it was taken.

Valen lifted the picture and inspected it closely. He stared as if expecting it to talk. He wondered when and where it was taken. It looked to be near the river. He smiled at the thought of Rhiannon keeping it by her side.

Rhiannon came back into the room. "So, I see you found one of my favorite photos."

Valen nodded as he placed the album back down on the table.

"I took it without you knowing during our second date. I've stared at it so many times, wondering where you were and what you were doing. And now, here you are standing in my living room," Rhiannon smiled softly.

Valen stood silent.

Rhiannon approached him and handed him his tea. She then pulled him down next to her on the couch and tucked her feet under his legs. Holding the cup of tea close to her lips, she sipped carefully. Valen watched her and smiled. She gave him such a sense of warmth and comfort that he never wanted to lose again.

"Rhiannon?"

"Yes?"

"Let's go away together."

"Valen, what are you talking about?"

"I want just you and me to go away. I've never been to Europe before, and I'd like to see all the sites. Whatcha' say? Will you go with me, and be my tour guide?"

Rhiannon laughed as if expecting Valen to be joking. "Valen, I have a job here. I can't just pick up and go."

"Why not? You just do it."

"Valen, be realistic. I just can't do that. I don't know what kind of world you've been living in, but you just don't leave a job all of a sudden to go site seeing. Besides, that takes a lot of money."

"Rhiannon, I haven't seen you in years, and quite frankly, I want your undivided attention. I want to be with you, just you. No work, nothing but you."

"Valen, I don't think I'm making myself clear," Rhiannon laughed in disbelief. "I can't. You've always been so spontaneous, which I love and admire, but Valen, life doesn't work that way."

"Life is how you want it to be, Rhiannon. It can be as spontaneous, or as planned as you want. All I know is that I want to live it to the fullest, spending every second as if it were my last. I want to continuously learn and experience more. That's the beauty of life, seeing, hearing, tasting, feeling, experiencing and learning. I'm not, haven't, nor ever will be stuck in one place, or profession. I'm just not made that way."

Rhiannon looked insulted.

"I'm not criticizing you," Valen quickly defended. "I'm not criticizing, or recommending my lifestyle to anyone. It's just how I live and how I see things. I could die any minute, and it scares me to death to think that I could have missed something by not being spontaneous enough. God has given us such a gift here on earth and we get to choose what we do with it. Well, I just don't want to waste it, and I don't want to waste another moment without you. Please Rhiannon, come with me. Let's travel, and see the world together."

Rhiannon was silenced by Valen's sincerity. She knew he was being foolish and unrealistic, but somehow she was being convinced. Perhaps she wanted to be. Inside she fought with her mind's sense of reality and her heart's sense of adventure.

"Valen, I agree with you. I do, but please be realistic. I can't just pick up and go. I have responsibilities here! Now, I'm sorry if you don't understand that. I made a commitment to those that hired me that I would do a good job. They trust me, and I won't let them down. That's called loyalty and being a person of your word. Maybe you've never had to give someone your word before, or maybe you have, but for me it means everything to stand-by your commitments and what you say."

"I understand," Valen said gently as he placed his full cup of tea down. "I know what I ask seems irresponsible, and I'm sorry. I also believe in one's word and being committed. I was just being blinded by my excitement. Perhaps some other time."

"Valen, you act as though you're never going to see me again. You're here in London with me right now. Why can't you just enjoy that. I am."

"I do Rhiannon, but I want more. Anyway, I don't know how long I'm going to be in London. I like it here, but I'm also ready to find a home, and I'm pretty sure it's not here."

"What are you talking about?" Rhiannon asked. "I thought you had a home."

"No, I left everything to come find you. I want you, Rhiannon. I always have."

"Valen, what are you saying?"

"Rhian, why do you think I came all this way?"

"I don't know. I guess I haven't given it much thought."

"Well, I came to find you. I've been without you too long, and my love hasn't diminished. I need you - I love you."

Rhiannon sat silent holding her cup tightly against her chest. Her mind was filled with flattery and joy. She had missed Valen and wanted to be with him, but this just seemed too fast. It seemed right and natural, but at the same time her mind couldn't come to terms with the rapidness of everything.

"Valen, I love you and always have, but this all seems so fast. I'm sorry, but I can't go away with you. I have responsibilities here, and it's just silly to leave. I'm sorry."

Once again, Valen felt the cold emptiness of heartache consume his body. It was a frightening yet familiar sensation, and his only response was to run from it.

"I understand," he said pridefully. "I had a great time tonight, thank you for joining me. Anyway, I should be going now." Valen stood and walked toward the door.

"Valen," Rhiannon stood and reached out for him. "Don't run."

"I'm not running. I just need to go. Goodnight."

The door closed softly behind him, and Rhiannon stood still. She knew she had hurt him, but she held strong to her position. He was being ridiculous.

"Crazy, just plain crazy," she thought to herself. "I can't just go away with him, what's he thinking?" Rhiannon's mind raced with thought. "But why am I staying here? What's here for me? A job I can barely tolerate, and a client that gives me the creeps? I must be crazy for choosing this life."

Rhiannon walked to the kitchen and slowly began a mundane cleaning process. She always started with the top of the stove, gently cleaning its surface. It never failed to help her think.

"Valen. I can't believe he came all this way for me. He's my dream, but he drives me so crazy. He's so irresponsible, or maybe it's me that's too responsible." Rhiannon cleaned her way to the kitchen sink. "I can't let him go. I need him, and I don't want to lose him again. I'm going to do it! I'm going to listen to my heart this time and satisfy it. My head's been running the show for too long. I'm tired of being lonely and without him." Rhiannon threw the dirty hand towel in the sink and ran toward the door. "I'm not letting him go again," she said aloud slamming the door behind her.

Valen was just entering his hotel room, when a man approached him. "Excuse me sir," the man said, "but I was hoping you could point me in the right direction?"

"I'll do my best, but I'm new to the city myself and..."

"Oh, I'm not new," the man interrupted, "I was hoping you could help me find a young woman by the name of Rhiannon."

"Rhiannon?" Valen asked puzzled. "Why do you ask?"

"Oh, I'm just an old friend, perhaps she's mentioned me," the man said as he extended his hand. "My name's Byron."

Valen took the man's hand hesitantly. "No, she's never mentioned you to me. I'm sorry." Valen got a weird feeling from the guy, as he shook his hand. It was almost as if he could see his soul, and it wasn't pretty.

"I don't think I can help you find her, either," Valen said. "I'm not sure where she lives myself."

"Awe, that's too bad," the man said sarcastically.

"Why would you assume I knew her anyway?" Valen asked.

"Call it a hunch," Byron said smiling.

"That's not good enough," Valen said abruptly. "Who are you, and what do you want?"

"Calm down, Mr. McCloud. As I said, I'm just a friend wondering if she's mentioned me?"

"And I told you she hasn't. If there's a problem, I'd like to settle it now."

"Now, now Mr. McCloud. You're going to get yourself all riled up for nothing. I'm sorry to have bothered you," Byron said as he turned to walk away.

"Wait a second," Valen said grabbing Byron's arm. "How do you know my name - who are you?"

"I told you," Byron said pulling his arm from Valen's grasp. "I'm a mutual friend. I work with Rhiannon on detailed information and was simply making sure that everything was proper. You know how sticky business relationships can get at times."

Valen looked solemn. "No, I don't," he replied.

"To any extend," Byron continued. "If you could tell Rhiannon I tried to stop by and to keep up the good work, I'd appreciate it."

"Sure," Valen replied, "But let me assure you that if any problems should arise, I'll know who to come to."

Byron walked off casually as if not threatened in the slightest, and Valen continued back to his room. A few minutes later, Rhiannon was at his door.

"Rhiannon? What are you doing here?"

A smile was spread across her face and her eyes were full of life. "I want to come with you," she said.

"But I thought you couldn't?"

"I know, but I changed my mind. I don't want to loose you again," Rhiannon cried hugging Valen's neck.

Valen stood silently just holding her, with his heart full.

The next morning, not a word was said. They were together again, and this time, nothing would separate them.

Valen was the first to break the silence. "Do you know a guy named, Byron?" He asked nonchalantly.

"Yes, that's my client here in England. My company sent me to take care of some tax issues with him. Why?"

"He paid me a little visit last night?"

"What? When?" Rhiannon said surprised jumping backward.

"Just before you came over. He met me outside my hotel. He knew my name and everything."

141

"Really? I can't believe it. What did he want?"

"Well, he said to tell you he stopped by and that you were doing a good job, but he kept asking if you had ever mentioned his name to me."

"I don't like this, Valen. I don't trust that guy."

"Who is he?"

"My client. In fact, he's the reason I'm over here. He owns a large distribution company, and my firm sent me over to assist him with some tax issues."

"Well, he acted really weird."

"He is. I thought he had a little crush on me, but this is ridiculous."

"Well, this seemed more than a crush. He was really interested to know if I knew anything about him."

"This isn't good, Valen. I've noticed some discrepancies with his taxes lately. I've stayed quiet, but now it's going too far."

"You think he's into something illegal?"

"Yes."

"Well, that makes sense, but I don't think you have anything to worry about. I think he was pretty much convinced that I didn't know a thing."

"Yea, but he may still want to talk to me. Valen, before we leave, I have to fix this, or it could follow me forever."

The next day, Rhiannon went to work as usual and met with Byron.

"How was your date?" he asked casually.

"Great. I met an old friend I haven't seen in quite a while. We grew up together."

"Really? I assume he told you about my little visit?"

"Yes he did. Which, I don't understand. Why would you do something like that?"

Byron stood up and walked over to Rhiannon confidently. "I deal with a lot of money, as you know, and I like to know what all my employees are doing."

"Well, with all due respect Byron, I'm not one of your employees, and you don't have the right to snoop around in my private life."

"Rhiannon. How can you talk to me that way," Byron smiled. "We're friends, besides nothing happened. You have to understand, I like to ensure safety." Byron said as he placed his hand on Rhiannon's shoulder.

Rhiannon stood abruptly, knocking his hand from her. "This is enough, Byron. Look, I was going to tell you this later, but now is better."

"What?" Byron asked.

"I'm leaving the firm. I'm just not enjoying the work anymore, and I've decided to pursue other interests. I've already informed my company and they will be providing you my replacement in the coming days. "

"Really?" Byron said seriously. "I thought we were having a good time."

"It's just time I took my leave."

"I see, well a lady must do what she must."

"I'm glad you see it that way," Rhiannon said extending her hand.

"Of course, Rhee," Byron said sarcastically. "Just make sure you keep everything to yourself. Understand." Byron said tightening his grip on her hand.

"It's against our confidentiality agreement to do otherwise," Rhiannon said calmly pretending not to be frightened, or in pain.

"Good. So long as we understand each other."

"We do," Rhiannon said as she turned to walk away.

"Oh Rhiannon," Byron shouted. "I've enjoyed working with you. Thank you for everything."

Rhiannon faked a smile as she waved good-bye from the elevator.

Rhiannon met Valen back at the hotel lobby.

"So, everything okay?" he asked.

"I hope so," she mumbled under her breath.

"What?" Valen asked.

"I mean, yep, everything is taken care of. Now, let's get out of here," she said taking Valen by the arm.

"You got it," Valen smiled as he waived down a cab.

"I can't believe I just quit my job," Rhiannon smirked. "This is crazy."

The two of them traveled most of Europe and enjoyed every second as if it were their last. Their love was so natural, so easy, that anyone watching them would be swept away into their world.

For the first time, Rhiannon looked forward to going to sleep. She had starting to dread it, because it only brought her closer to tomorrow and the same day-to-day rituals she had to perform in order to get by. But now, she felt full of purpose and couldn't wait for tomorrow.

Valen held her tightly in his arms and cradled her as he had always done. They created a world of their own - a false sense of freedom, far from any imprisoning type rules and responsibility.

By the fourth day of their travels, Valen felt compelled to share his secret with Rhiannon. He wanted her to know about his money. Not for impression, but because he wanted her to know everything. He wanted her to know that he had never even looked at another women since her and that even though he had accomplished his dream, it was still incomplete without her. He wanted to ask her to marry him. Valen traveled to Europe for this purpose. He had the ring, and he was ready for her to have it. It had been hidden away too long.

Valen had been routinely pulling it from its case to gaze at its sparkle. He dreamed of the day it would embrace Rhiannon's finger with his promise. Now, the time had come.

Their travels had brought them to Venice, and Valen knew there could be no more perfect time, or place, to ask Rhiannon to marry him.

That evening, while overlooking the canals of Venice from their hotel room balcony, Valen whispered in her ear. "I have something to tell you."

Rhiannon closed her eyes in anticipation of Valen's words. "What?" she whispered.

"When we were separated, and I was living at that beach I told you about...,"

"Yes?"

"Well, I started my own business."

"Really," Rhiannon turned smiling. "That's great! It's what you always wanted!"

"Yes. Yes it was, and it paid off very well."

"Well, I thought something must of paid off by the way you've been spoiling me lately," Rhiannon laughed. "What kind of company is it?"

"A greeting card company."

"Oh, Valen that's great! I'm so proud of you. I knew you would do it!" she shouted hugging his neck.

"Yea, it was great. I made the cards from the photos and poems I created, but that's not the best part."

146

"Well, what else could it be?" Rhiannon beamed.

"A larger company bought me out."

"What?" Rhiannon's expression suddenly grew to shock.

"Yep. They bought Imaginations, my company, for a lot of money."

"Valen - Are you serious?"

"Very."

Again, Rhiannon threw her arms around his neck. "Congratulations," she whispered. "I knew you would do it. I knew you could do it!"

"But that's still not all," Valen smiled.

"What else could there be?" Rhiannon laughed in disbelief.

Valen reached out for Rhiannon's neck and touched the cross he had given her. Then, he looked into her eyes and felt as though he was peering into her soul. He could feel her looking back. It felt right.

Kneeling on one knee, Valen presented the ring from his pocket and placed it gently around her finger.

"Will you marry me?"

Valen's voice carried firm and sincere, and it made Rhiannon's heart stop. She gasped for air and as a thousand emotions flooded her body, she began to cry.

"Yes," she cried. "Yes!"

Valen stood to meet her embrace, and she held him tightly against her. Neither spoke, but simply savored the other's touch.

"I love you, Valen."

"And I love you. I promise to make you happy, Rhiannon...always."

Rhiannon couldn't stop the tears.

And both awaited a new tomorrow.

Chapter XV

The delight of trying foreign cuisines excited Valen's senses. He loved the exotic smells and rich flavors, and so he eagerly awaited their upcoming trip to Germany.

Upon arriving, Rhiannon and Valen also savored as many of the historic castles Germany had to offer. They were struck by the more relaxed pace many of the people seemed to enjoy and how making personal connections and engaging in casual conversations over food and drink seemed to be their most favored pastime. This compared to the hurried lifestyles they were accustomed to was a welcomed indulgence.

Rhiannon however, wanted to visit London once more. That's where she felt the most inspired. So, without hesitation, Valen agreed to Rhiannon's request, and the next morning they loaded the train and headed back to Rhiannon's apartment. For there was a lot of planning and packing to do.

As they began the arduous task of loading all of Rhiannon's belongings into boxes, she began to cry.

"What's wrong?" Valen asked.

"I'm just so very happy," Rhiannon smiled. "I can't believe we're going to spend the rest of our lives together. It's all I ever really wanted, and I guess I just now realized that."

Valen rubbed his hands through her hair. "It's what I always wanted too, and I've always known that," he smiled softly. "You have always been my inspiration and heart."

Highways End

After a few hours had past, Valen's stomach reminded him that it was time to eat. "Are you hungry?" He asked.

"Starved."

"Any recommendations as to where we should go?"

"Yes, as a matter of fact I do. Com'on, let's go. I'll surprise you."

"You got it."

Rhiannon smiled and looked at Valen coyly as they approached an ancient, run-down building. It was about five stories tall and built completely of wood. It was obviously old and looked as if it came straight out of a Charles Dickens' story. The various aromas that came from the kitchen were marvelous though, and Valen's stomach growled in agreement.

"I don't know how you stay so fit. If I ate the way you do, I'd be as big as a house," Rhiannon smiled. "Com'on, it tastes even better than it smells."

The place was owned and run by a slender French woman with hard features and a weathered face, but through her eyes, her true nature was revealed. They radiated joy, and when one looked into them they were almost blinding with light.

"Nous avons des vins," Valen stammered.

"Oui, monsieur," the lady said smiling as she walked away. "I'll be right back, and thanks for trying to speak my beautiful language – but no more, please."

Rhiannon laughed and reached out for Valen's hand. "I love you," she whispered. "You make me happier than I ever thought

150

possible - thank you."

Valen squeezed her hand and looked at the ring. He couldn't believe it was finally on her finger. It was even more beautiful than he had imaged.

Shortly thereafter, the old woman arrived with their bottle of wine. "I brought out our house Merlot," she said as she opened the bottle. "I hope you like it."

Valen twirled the glass just a little and took a slight sniff. The wine danced with fruitful aroma, and as he tasted, it nipped his tongue and left it dry.

"Very, good," he said.

The woman poured Rhiannon's glass and then filled the rest of Valen's to the rim.

Valen gestured for Rhiannon to order, but just before she spoke, the woman interrupted.

"Ah," she nodded. "You trusted me with the wine, and now I ask that you trust me with the food, Uh?"

Rhiannon looked toward Valen in agreement.

"Sure," he nodded reluctantly.

"Good. I'll be back shortly then. It'll be worth the wait. I promise," the woman smiled.

Valen's eyes took in the interior of the room, admiring the antique decor. The only other occupant was an old skinny man sipping soup from a bowl and reading the local paper. The room was filled with clutter, but in an arranged sort of way. There was a sweet scent of aged wood and old photographs decorated the walls. Valen felt as if he were in the woman's house. There were no other waiters available, and for a moment Valen wondered if it was her house.

The woman later arrived with a platter filled with a wonderful assortment of foods. There were fresh vegetables, breads, cheeses, various meats and sauces. It wasn't the sort of thing Valen usually enjoyed. He liked the big hearty meals, but the woman's face was filled with such joy, that he couldn't refuse.

"Looks great," he smiled.

Rhiannon knowing Valen's true feelings just grinned. She loved eating like this. Her first pick was the sliced carrot. She dipped it in the homemade dressing and rolled her eyes with contentment.

"Com'on and dig in. It's good for you."

Valen strained a smile and headed straight for the bread and cheese.

After their meal, Valen felt surprisingly full. "That wasn't too bad," he said placing his hand on Rhiannon's.

Their stomachs were full. They were warm, and everything for the first time in both their lives felt right. Valen laughed aloud as he thought of how he had made his fortune doing what he loved, how he was now enjoying the cuisines of a foreign land and had the woman of his dreams by his side. Things were definitely going well.

"Did you enjoy your dinner?" The woman asked.

"Yes. It was all very delicious. Thank you," Valen replied. "Perhaps another glass of wine?" He suggested, but the woman just looked at him and smiled.

"No more - now enough with the drinking. You go enjoy each other and this world without so much of da' drink. It can and will catch up with you - okay?"

The tone of her voice, the look in her eyes and the way she smiled at him, made Valen feel something very convicting. Something he frankly had never felt before. He saw in her a story of a lost love. Although her eyes danced today, he seemed to see the scars of a past that told of over-indulgences, mistakes and regrets.

"Yes, m'am," was all he could think to say.

As they shuffled from the restaurant, Rhiannon looked at Valen noticing something was on his mind. "You okay?" she asked.

Valen, not ready to make any admissions of his thoughts about the woman and what he felt she saw in him, redirected his attentions back to Rhiannon.

"Just thinking," he smiled, looking around at the damp cobblestone streets softly lit under the lights. "It's a beautiful night, but look up there. I think a storm cloud may be coming our way."

"Good, let's go back to the hotel and enjoy it," she smiled.

Walking down the street, passing smiles were shared by other lovers lost in embracing strolls. Suddenly, Rhiannon stopped and turned to Valen.

"Let's go home," she said.

"We were...I thought?"

"No, I mean let's go back to the states and find us a place to live, sooner than we planned. I'm ready, Valen. I can't wait to start my life with you. I want a home. A place where my stuff is in one place with yours."

Valen smiled, gently kissing the soft curve of her nose just between the eyes. "That's my spot you know."

"What?" Rhiannon laughed.

"This spot right here," as he kissed her again. "See how my lips fit just right."

"You cheese," Rhiannon laughed. "Now, seriously. What do you think?" she said playfully pushing him in urgency.

"I think it's a good idea. I'm ready, but what about the wedding."

"Oh, no!" Rhiannon shouted playfully hitting Valen's shoulder. "I've been so caught up, I haven't even called my mom yet!"

The rain started softly, but soon cascaded into a full-blown storm. They ran through the downpour and rested under the first overhang they could find. Stopping under a cafe's umbrella, Valen pulled Rhiannon close and kissed her. She was beautiful even soaking wet. They held each other until the storm subsided a little and then continued their jog to the apartment.

"Being with you seems to make everything different," Rhiannon said as they reached her apartment. "Even a storm becomes a memory I want to relive."

As they made their way into the bedroom, Valen snuck behind her as she passed by the bed and playfully tripped her onto it.

"You slug!" she laughed. "Com'on," she said jumping on the bed, gesturing the pose of a boxer. "I'll take you on."

Valen jumped to the challenge and soon they were wrestling all across the room. With Valen locked down under Rhiannon's knees, he begged for mercy. "You win," he laughed.

"Of course I do," she said coyly. "Now, I'm going to call my mother," as she strutted to the phone.

Rhiannon dialed the number, but got a disconnected recording. Assuming she dialed the wrong number, she tried again, but got the same message.

"No answer?" Valen asked.

"No, the number's disconnected," she said puzzled. "I don't understand."

"Well, maybe they got a private line. You remember all the solicitation calls and hang-ups your house used to get. Maybe your mom got tired of it and changed the number."

"I doubt it. Most of those hang-ups were from Pete's affairs, so even if they did change the number, I'm sure those girls would have the new one," Rhiannon said sarcastically.

"I'm sure everything's fine. Don't let your imagination get carried away."

"I'm not Valen, but this is weird. I would've at least thought someone would've contacted me."

"And I'm sure they will," Valen walked over and put his arm around her. "It'll be okay. Have you heard anything about your brother, Chris lately?" He asked somewhat attempting to change the subject to keep Rhiannon from worrying.

Rhiannon knowing what he was trying to do went along with it. "Chris is still...Chris. A bundle of smiles, hugs and love. Mom said he may even have a crush on a girl," unable to change her concern, Rhiannon continued, "Valen, I'm telling you something is wrong at home. I mean, I just spoke with mother last week..."

Again changing the subject, Valen interjected. "A girlfriend?" Valen smiled. "No kidding. Good for him. I guess he's old enough now."

"Yeah. He's seventeen and quite the charmer," Rhiannon said aggravated with Valen's attempts to change topics.

"Wow - I remember him running around the house and playing hiding-go-seek like it was yesterday."

I think so. He's apparently doing the best in his class, which makes my Mom happy," Rhiannon smiled.

"That's great, Rhiannon. It really is. It'll be good to see your mom and brother again."

Rhiannon looked in thought, "Yea, it will," she smiled. "I'm going to try the number again."

"Here, give me the phone. Let me dial this time. It's all in the wrist, you know." Valen gestured with a smile. "See, I told you so. It's ringing. You must have been in a hurry and misdialed. Here," he smiled handing her the phone.

Rhiannon quickly grabbed the phone out of Valen's hands and was relieved to hear her mother's voice. "I'm coming home, Momma, and I have a wonderful surprise for you. Valen and I are getting married!" Valen could hear her mother's shout of joy clear across the room.

Knowing it was going to be awhile before Rhiannon got off the phone, Valen headed to the couch, smiling, and comforted by his soon-to-be wife's excitement.

Highways End

Chapter XVI

After a few weeks past, everything was finally packed and ready to go. Rhiannon's office didn't want to lose her talents and therefore made every attempt and accommodation imaginable to try and keep her on the team, including paying for movers to send her stuff back to the states.

Rhiannon reluctantly, but graciously agreed to accept the firm's offer to take an extended leave of absence for the time being, but knew she would most likely never return to the fast-paced life she was now eager to leave. She had lost herself in her work while trying to find herself through work. Now, she felt that perhaps she could find what she was missing with Valen. However, this too was a misguided hope. For she had yet to discover that true fulfillment cannot be found in any occupation, position, possession, or person. Instead, purpose is found at a much higher level. Both Rhiannon and Valen would soon discover this truth.

Hours later they were loading a plane, sitting first class. Being a long flight, they spent most of the hours laughing and eating, but Valen did manage to write a little in his journal. He had neglected it for a while now, and his mind struggled with capturing the words in his heart. However, in time, his pen began racing once again.

Rhiannon preoccupied herself with various copies of inflight magazines.

By the time the plane landed in Atlanta, both were exhausted. So, they skipped a formal dinner and went straight to the hotel.

Highways End

The next morning Rhiannon tried to call her Mom to let her know they would be driving into town soon, but again, she received a disconnected signal. "Okay, I must be stupid and dialing this number wrong every time I try home. Here, you try," she grunted as she threw the phone to Valen.

"I don't know. I'm getting the same recording you are now." Valen stated.

"This is crazy. Com'on, you ready? We're driving down there now," she said flinging her luggage over her left shoulder.

They arrived at Rhiannon's old house around noon, but found it abandoned. No one could be found anywhere, and a lock was on the door. "We just spoke to her not that long ago. What is going on! I don't like this, Valen." Rhiannon said sternly.

Immediately, she ran to the neighbors and banged their door.

"Mr. and Mrs. Wright! Mr. and Mrs. Wright! Please! Open the door! It's Rhiannon!" she cried.

Slowly, Mrs. Wright opened the door. A frightful woman by nature, she was offset by Rhiannon's hysteria.

"Please, Mrs. Wright...do you know where my family is?"

The old woman looked to the ground. "Yes, child. Come in."

Valen and Rhiannon sat at the coffee table and awaited Mrs. Wright's arrival from the kitchen.

Carrying three sweet teas, the old woman sat and prepared herself to release the bad news.

Rhiannon sat impatiently, not touching her drink.

"Rhiannon, my dear. Your mother, brother and step-father...," she hesitated.

"Yes?" Rhiannon said fearfully. "Please, I have to know."

"They were recently in a tragic car accident."

"Oh, no," Valen sighed.

Rhiannon sat silent, without expression.

"Pete was driving and tried to pass a tractor over a hill and before they realized it, another truck was on top of them. They didn't have time to react, from what I understand. Your family died immediately, Rhiannon. I'm sorry." The old woman reached over to take Rhiannon's hand. "The driver that hit them is still in critical care at the hospital."

Rhiannon remained silent and in shock.

"We tried to track you down, but no one could get in touch with you. You're obviously next-of-kin, but the house was locked up until you were contacted - and your father's attorney began steps to help settle the estate. Here's his information," she said as she passed his card over to her.

Valen held Rhiannon tight, but she pushed him off and walked out the door.

"Thank you, Mrs. Wright," Valen sighed.

"Give the child my best, will you, and let her know that her family is resting at Honor Cemetery. Arrangements were made when she could not be contacted...she's such a sweet girl. Please, take good care of her."

"I will m'am," Valen said softly as he walked out to find Rhiannon.

Half way to her home Rhiannon broke down. The thought of her mother and brother dead was too hard to handle. Especially after she had just spoken with her. It was all so fast and sudden. Rhiannon's mind raced with confusion.

Valen stood back and watched Rhiannon fall to her knees. He didn't know if he should intrude, or let her have her time. With tears filling his eyes, he gazed at the old house remembering the first time he drove up the gated driveway on his bike. He remembered how fresh and beautiful Rhiannon was, how elegant her mother was, and how cheerful and alive Christopher was. Then, his memory flashed to the reality before him. Rhiannon was broken, and her family was gone. Valen began to walk hesitantly toward her, but then decided to turn and walk a little ways down the street. He knew she wanted to be alone.

Valen circled the block and thought. His mind raced with images of the past, all he had seen in such a short time. He thought how full life was, how gorged with activity and how, in an instant, it can all be taken away. Thirty minutes later found him back at the drive of Rhiannon's home.

Rhiannon was now rested on the porch swing, rocking. Her eyes still full of sorrow, she tried to smile. "Hi," she whispered.

"Hi," Valen sighed. "How ya' doin'?"

"Not good."

Valen walked the stairs slowly and sat beside her. Rhiannon laid her head on his lap.

"I can't believe this has happened," she cried.

Valen sat silent and brushed her hair gently with his hand.

"It seems like yesterday that I lived here, you know? I can still see their faces and feel as though they will be coming up the drive any second," Rhiannon rambled. Suddenly, she shot up quickly in frustration. "I can't believe God would let this happen. What kind of God is he? Christopher and my mom were good people," she shouted looking at Valen. "Why?"

Valen looked into Rhiannon's eyes and met her soul. "I don't know Rhiannon, but I can tell you that I don't think God tried to hurt you. I know you don't see it now and that you don't want to hear it, but I do believe everything happens for a reason. No matter how tragic, no matter how awful, I have to believe that through it all, there's a valuable lesson learned, that something positive can come out of it."

Rhiannon stood and walked the length of the porch. "Oh, stop with your philosophical B.S.! What do you know? They weren't your family."

"I do know, Rhiannon. I've seen and dealt with more death and tragedy than I like to admit, and the only way I've gotten through it all is holding on to the thread of belief that it all has a purpose. Sherman demonstrated that to me. Granted, I've done a poor job of taking God seriously, but in my heart I do believe, and..."Valen hesitated in mid-sentence as if something struck him upside the head.

Rhiannon looked at him with curiosity. "What, Valen? What is it?"

"I feel sick," he said softly. "I don't feel well at all. I'm sorry."

Valen was facing the reality that he had been running. God was not a symbol, not a good luck charm and not a philosophy of life. He was God, and He wanted nothing but Valen's complete devotion void of worldly distraction. It was a truth and conviction in his soul that could not be ignored.

Rhiannon sighed and walked over to the stairs. Valen remained on the swing, trying to collect himself and his composure. They both sat silent in the sun's flaming descent.

As the street lights turned on, Valen walked over and extended his hand out to Rhiannon.

"Come on," he said softly. "Let's go."

Rhiannon looked up at him with empty eyes. "Where?" she said.

"To say good-bye."

Rhiannon walked over to the car, grabbed her sweater and looked at Valen.

"Well, let's go," he urged softly.

Rhiannon and Valen walked briskly under the moon's soft light. Upon approaching the graveyard, Rhiannon stopped.

It was an old graveyard, and resembled the kind seen in horror films. It had rusted iron gates, toppled and cracked tombstones and ancient trees, but its grounds were kept immaculate. In fact, because of its civil war occupants and broad history, it was one of the most expensive and honored places to be buried.

Rhiannon knew exactly where her family's plots were. Years earlier, Rhiannon went with her parents as they picked their grave sites. She thought it awkward and morbid at the time, but after the death of her father, she had grown more mature with the concept and reality of death.

Valen walked hand-in-hand with Rhiannon as they approached the two freshly dug graves. Peter didn't have a site. He had been cremated and buried in his hometown of Baton Rouge, Louisiana. Elizabeth and Christopher were buried next to Liz's ex-husband and Rhiannon's father, Cane.

Under the moon's hypnotic glow, Valen read the phrase that all three of the headstones had borrowed from a poem once read:

They charted separated courses through rough waters and met at the waters' edge. Now, they live forever, never to be parted again.

Tears rolled from Rhiannon's eyes, dampening the fresh dirt over her mother's grave. Memories flooded her mind, and confusion filled her heart, yet somehow she began to feel stronger. She could still feel her mother's presence - her love.

Rhiannon then knelt beside Chris' grave. She rubbed the tombstone softly with her hand and looked toward the stars. She thought of where he was now and smiled. Deep in her soul, she believed too, and knew his laughter and glow would last forever now.

Rhiannon stood and walked over to Valen who was alone with his thoughts. He was reading several of the tombstones and reflecting on life. He thought how fast it could all be taken away. And he wondered if these people had the chance to do it all over again, would they? And would they do it differently? He thought how most people simply take life for granted, assuming the gift will last forever. So, they spend years chasing the wind. They reside to live out their days in jobs they tolerate at best and invest decades in struggling as victims to their situations and circumstances. Immediately, Valen pulled the tiny notebook from his pocket and scratched down his thoughts.

"Whatcha' doin'?" Valen heard Rhiannon say softly behind him.

"Just thinking how fast life can be taken' away," he said snapping his fingers.

"I know," she said touching his shoulder. "So, let's go and begin ours," she smiled.

Valen turned with compassion filled eyes. "Is everything okay? Are you sure you're ready to go?"

"I'm fine, and so is my family. I'm ready."

That night was spent with a friend of the family, Frank Bonner. He had worked for Rhiannon's father as a contractor and had known Rhiannon ever since she was born. He was now an old man, widowed several years earlier. He was an honest man, and his hands were worn and tired, and his eyes hung low, but his kindness knew no bounds. Knowing their grief, he thought it best to leave them alone. So, he simply made them a dinner of hot beef stew, showed them to their separate bedrooms and then retired to his own.

"I'll be gettin' up early in the mornin'," Frank said. "So, take whatever time you need gettin' ready."

"Thank you, Frank," Rhiannon smiled. "We appreciate it."

"Not to mention it," Frank said gruffly. "Now, make yourself at home, and may God bless you," he said changing to a soft and gentle tone.

Neither Rhiannon nor Valen slept well that night, too many thoughts were going through their heads. Reality seemed to have crashed down in front of them. The mixed emotions they felt were maddening. They were facing tremendous loss and sorrow, but at the same time, they were happier than they had ever been due to their upcoming marriage and the unveiling truth around them.

Valen tip-toed out of his room and tapped on Rhiannon's door.

She opened the door smiling,"I think it's better this way don't you?"

Valen knew what she meant. "Yes. It's a bit old fashioned, but yes. It is better this way. Can we talk for a minute before I scurry back to my room?" Valen smiled.

"Sure. Come on in," Rhiannon peaked out in the hall like a little child about to be caught with her hand in a cookie jar.

"So, what kind of wedding do you think we should have?" Valen said breaking the silence.

"I don't know, but I assume a big one's out of the question. Friends and family are few..." Rhiannon hesitated with remembrance of her family, but soon regained composure. "I think we should have a quiet, low-key wedding.

"That sounds nice...it's just you and me kid," Valen smiled, pulling her closer.

"I know of just the place to have it too," Rhiannon smiled. "I've heard of people driving out to this old garden store north of town to wed. The owners apparently perform weddings there."

"What?" Valen laughed.

"Seriously, some preacher and his wife own this quaint store that sells flowers, plants, bird-feeders and even some gardening tools. I hear it's very charming and cozy. Anyway, I think it would suit us just fine."

"Sounds interesting. Let's do it! Let's go get married in a tool shed." And together they laughed.

Early the next morning, Rhiannon made a phone call to her father's attorney settling the estate and provided details for the next steps to be taken, including selling the family home.

Her next call was to the garden store.

"Peacock Nursery," a raspy old voice answered.

"Reverend Peacock?"

"Yes 'm. Hows can I help ya'?"

"Well, my name is Rhiannon Waters, and I was wondering if you still conducted ceremonies at your store?"

"Sure do, just had one yesterday, matter fact."

"Great! Well, me and my fiancée were hoping to get married."

"That right? Well, congratulations child! When were you hoping to set the date?"

"As soon as possible, really. It will just be the two of us."

"Yes, m'am. Well, I have time later today, if you'd like. We still have all the decorations up from yesterday," he replied gently.

"That would be great, Reverend. Thank you."

"My pleasure m'am. How's three o'clock sound?"

"Perfect! We'll see you then."

"Oh, wait child. What's the groom's name?"

"Valen. Valen McCloud."

"Okay, see ya' later, and dress anyway you'd like," he said.

Rhiannon could barely hang up the phone she was so excited. She jumped to tell Valen the good news. "Valen!" she shouted running throughout the house.

Valen was outside sitting on the steps smoking a cigarette. "Out here," he replied exhaling.

"And where did you get that?" Rhiannon teased.

"Found a pack in my luggage, but it doesn't taste so good anymore. I don't know, I just feel like something's changing in me. In a good way, I suppose." Valen flung the cigarette and looked at Rhiannon. "Kind of like sleeping in separate rooms felt right too.

169

You know what I mean?"

Rhiannon poised herself gently beside him and looked deep into his eyes. "Yes. I do," she smiled.

She continued. "Good news. I talked to the preacher down at the gardening store."

"Really? What'd he say?"

"Well, how's three o'clock today sound?"

"You're kidding?"

"No, he said he could do it today. Can you believe it? I'm so excited!"

"Well, we'd better get some wedding rings fast," Valen nudged.

"Yes, but if we can't find what we're looking for today, it's still okay, Valen. We'll still be married, and I'll still have you. And we'll have a lifetime to go shopping for rings."

"You're right. We can get them anytime. So, now that that's out of the way, what do you wear at a tool shed wedding?" he laughed.

"It's a garden store, not a tool shed," Rhiannon smiled, playfully slapping Valen's arm. "I was told to wear whatever," she continued. "So, to make this thing even more interesting, I thought we could both wear our overalls," she smiled.

"I guess I don't see why not? Sounds fun. I just can't wait to be your husband," Valen said kissing her cheek.

The remainder of the day was spent cleaning Frank's house, packing the car and getting dressed. Three o'clock arrived before either one of them knew it.

Valen thought about calling his brother to see how he was doing, but he had forgotten the number. So, he thought about stopping by his old house instead. It wasn't far. So, as Rhiannon dressed, Valen made his way out to the old man's garage. Inside, he found a rusted 1959 Pontiac. The keys hung from the ignition. Quickly, he jumped in and sped towards his old home.

Saddened, but unsurprised, he found the house closed and boarded-up. There was no sign of his brother. Perhaps he moved on, or perhaps he was dead. Valen realized he may never know, and although sad, a piece of him was okay not knowing. He appreciated the sacrifices his brother had made for him, and knew life had taken its toll on him. He was young when so much responsibility had landed on his shoulders. Even though the two of them had never been close, Valen loved his brother and appreciated all he had done, despite his imperfections. So, wherever his brother was, he wished him well and as he drove away, he whispered aloud, "thank you."

Valen made his way back to Rhiannon without her even knowing he was gone.

"I'm starving," Rhiannon said as he walked into the bedroom.

"Me too, but let's grab something after the service. I can't wait. Did you call the cab?"

"Of course. In fact, he's pulling up now," she signaled out the bedroom window.

"Make sure to leave the thank you note," Rhiannon shouted as she made her way to the cab with baggage under tow.

"I'm doing that as we speak," Valen responded, tucking an extra hundred dollars in the envelope to express his appreciation.

As they pulled up the dirt drive to Peacock Nursery, dust filled the air. "Look at this place," Valen laughed. "It looks to be over a hundred years old."

"I think it is, but how often do you get to marry the man of your dreams in a hundred year old hardware store. I wouldn't pass this up if you paid me."

As they walked in they were astounded with its appearance. Mr. Peacock's wife really had the place decorated well.

Hay barrels were placed throughout the store and an assortment of wild flowers and plants were strategically placed on the walls and ceilings. Scattered on the floor, starting from the walkway and ending at a podium, were bright red, yellow and white rose petals. The place looked like an old barn that had exploded with color. It was uniquely beautiful.

"Well, well, this must be the happy couple." A large heavyset man said limping out from behind the back.

"Yes, sir. My name's Valen and this is Rhiannon," Valen replied extending his hand.

"Nice to meet you, Valen. My name's John and this lovely lady," he said pointing to the elegant older woman standing behind him, "is my wife, Clara."

"Nice to meet you both," she said softly.

"Oh, Mrs. Peacock, the place is beautiful. You didn't have to go to so much trouble."

"It was no trouble at all. In fact, I enjoy doing it. It always reminds me of our wedding," she said patting John lovingly on his belly.

John was a burley looking man, with a thick, solid white beard. He resembled a giant, and his eyes were as dark as coal. His voice was heavy and thundersome, but his kindness and warmth was apparent from the start. He was dressed in his Sunday suit, but appeared strangled by his tie. He stood with his worn Bible in one hand and a marriage certificate in the other and was ready to begin the ceremony immediately.

"Clara, are you ready to witness for these two fine people?"

"Absolutely," she said smiling compassionately at both Rhiannon and Valen. "You're a beautiful couple."

Clara was dressed in an off-white summer dress and radiated with beauty. She was just slightly shorter than John and carried herself in a stately manner. Valen thought how she resembled delicate crystal, fragile to the touch. Her eyes were sky blue and her hair tightly pulled back in a bun. Hints of her once flowing brown hair showed through her dark gray, and her skin appeared softer than silk. She was an elegant woman, and it was apparent that her younger beauty once rivaled the landscapes around her.

Clara helped situate Valen and Rhiannon in their proper places and then took her rehearsed position behind the bride. John smiled brightly and began with the marriage vows.

173

"We are gathered here together today to join these two in holy matrimony under God's love and blessing. Love is a gift from heaven and must be treated as such. It is a gift that must not be neglected, but nourished. May your love for one another always be a strength and a glue that binds you forever, but to never take position over your relationship with our Lord and Savior, Jesus Christ. For a strand of three is not easily broken and may Christ always be the center of your life, binding you together with Him. So that as you grow closer to Him, He draws you closer together."

The Reverend spoke with such power and conviction that both Rhiannon and Valen stood embraced by his voice. They looked at one another and smiled at the honesty of the situation. They had dreamed of this day ever since they met and at that instant, all of their life experiences blended together to create an inner strength and appreciation for this moment more powerful than both could express.

"Do you Valen take Rhiannon to be your wife? To have and to hold until death do you part?"

"I do," he said softly, holding Rhiannon's hand tightly.

"Do you Rhiannon take Valen as your husband? To have and to hold until death do you part?"

"I do," she sighed, wiping a tear from her eye.

"Then, with the powers vested in me, I now pronounce you husband and wife. You may kiss the bride."

Valen placed his hand to Rhiannon's angelic face and pulled her close to him. He kissed her soft and unlike ever before. He felt his knees buckle. Valen could hardly stand from the flows of emotion running through him, and he felt Rhiannon tremble the same. The kiss was short, but the most meaningful they ever shared.

Rhiannon glanced back and smiled at Clara. She was holding a worn handkerchief and crying endlessly. Reverend Peacock gestured for Rhiannon and Valen to turn around. "May I present to you, Mr. and Mrs. Valen McCloud."

Three people made up the congregation, one being Mrs. Peacock, who stood crying and clapping enthusiastically. The remaining two were small children, seated in the very back. They were covered with dirt and cheered excitedly as Valen and Rhiannon made their exit hand-in-hand. One of the children reached out and handed Rhiannon a wrapped gift. "It's from all of us," she smiled shyly.

"Why, thank you," Rhiannon smiled joyfully.

The cab was waiting for them out front with the ignition turned on and air-condition blowing. Valen walked Rhiannon over to the passenger's side and opened her door. He waved a salute of thanks to the Peacocks, fastened his seatbelt and directed the cab to the nearest rental car agency.

The only car available at the agency was a baby blue minivan, which actually worked out perfectly to hold all of Rhiannon's luggage.

Halfway out of town, Rhiannon showed Valen the gift they had received from the children. "Look," she said with surprise. "A leather Bible with THE MCCLOUD FAMILY engraved on it. And it's from the Peacocks. How sweet of them." Suddenly she shouted aloud, "Oh, no - We forgot to pay them!"

"Pay who? I just paid for the car? What do you mean?" Valen queried.

"No, no. Mr. and Mrs Peacock. I don't remember us paying them!"

"Don't worry. I took care of that too," Valen said calmly.

Miles down the road John and Clara were cleaning up their shop. "You know, that was a nice couple," John smiled.

"They all are," Clara agreed.

John reached in his pocket for his handkerchief, but surprisingly pulled out an envelope instead.

"What's that honey?" Clara asked John as he tore it open.

"I don't know, but I guess we'll find out soon enough," he said.

Inside, was a letter from Valen along with a check for several thousand dollars. The note simply read,

> "Now, you can continue on.
>
> Thank you for your kindness.
>
>   Sincerely,
>
>   Valen and Rhiannon"

"What is this?" John stood holding the check. His face flushed.

"What do you think he meant by, now you can continue?" Clara whispered peering over John's shoulder.

John looked at the sign posted behind him and smiled. "God bless him. And somehow he knew exactly how much we needed." he whispered looking up to heaven with understanding.

Earlier, before the wedding started, as Rhiannon and Valen were pulling up to the store, Valen noticed a foreclosure sign tossed carelessly to the side of the building. Valen could tell the Peacocks were in financial trouble and yet, they stood with smiles on their faces and didn't ask a penny for their services. The children that had attended the wedding were a couple of kids from down the street. Their home life was one of neglect, with both parents never at home. The Peacocks helped them out quietly, by making sure they were fed and had a safe place to play. Valen's gift was one of compassion and gratitude and was never discussed.

Back on the road, Valen and Rhiannon had no idea where they were going. They had been on vacation for weeks, and so, a honeymoon seemed irrelevant. Instead, they decided to find a home. They had to first drop off their rental car and so, Valen thought it a good idea to first travel to Samuel's place, pick up his old bike, and at the same time, introduce him to Rhiannon.

By memory, Valen took the same familiar highway he had traveled years earlier. This time however, instead of being beaten and poor, he had accomplished all his dreams. Images of what were, flashed through his memory as they drove down the desolate highway. Rhiannon's seat was laid back, and she was fast asleep. It was just Valen, the radio, the wind in his hair and the endless highway. He wondered if Samuel had changed at all since he left. He hoped that he was well. He hadn't heard from him since he left, so he assumed everything was fine. After hours of driving, the highway ended in the old seaport Valen once called home.

Nothing much had changed since he'd been gone. The boats still looked the same, the docks were still stained with salt and blood, and all the men there were hard as ever. Valen turned to wake Rhiannon.

"Rhian, wake up."

Rhiannon rose slowly. "Where are we?"

"Well, this is where I used to call home," Valen said gesturing to the landscape.

Rhiannon looked around with disgust. "You're kidding."

"Nope."

"My mind had it pictured to be something more exotic."

"Well, it is pretty exotic," Valen smiled.

"No. You know what I mean, more beachy," Rhiannon said waving her hands for expression.

"I know, but it does have its pretty parts. I promise."

"Samuel still here?" Rhiannon asked.

"I don't know, but we're gonna find out," he said climbing from the car. "Come on."

Valen took Rhiannon's hand as they walked down to the main

dock. Men, stained with dirt and sun, stood aimlessly around the docks. Some were drunk, others fishing. Valen passed the old bar he used to frequent with a quick glance, shook his head in disbelief and headed straight for the sand.

"Com'on take your shoes off," he said sliding off his boots.

"The sand's hot?" Rhiannon asked.

"Naw, you get used to it, I promise. If not, I'll carry you."

Men shouted as Rhiannon knelt over to undo her laces.

"Lookin' good babe!" One man bellowed.

"Ignore 'em. Most of these guys are harmless," Valen said reassuringly.

"Anyway, my and Samuel's old place is right down here." Valen pointed down the beach. "Just beyond that fallen tree there."

As they reached the house, they saw it was abandoned.

"Looks like it's been deserted for a while," Rhiannon said brushing her hair from her face.

"Looks like it. I'm gonna go in, though. You're welcome to stay here if you'd like."

"I don't think so," she said sarcastically glancing over her shoulder at the men still shouting.

The house had been empty for some time by the looks of it. Dust and sand had gathered all over and some windows had been knocked out.

"Well, I guess I should've stayed in better touch with Samuel. There's no telling where he is now."

"Can you believe this is where it all happened for me?" He said shaking his head. "It's unbelievable how and where some things get their start."

Rhiannon smiled. "I know," she said reaching for his hand.

"I hope Samuel still has my bike. We gotta' find him."

"Come on," he said walking back up the beach. "I know where to look."

Valen headed straight back to the bar. If Sam wasn't there the guys inside would definitely know where to find him.

"Sammy and I used to hang out in this dump."

"Cover your ears, there are some nasty things in here," he said pulling Rhiannon closer.

As they walked in, all eyes turned to gaze at the vision standing to Valen's left. Rhiannon was the only woman there. It was growing dusk, and the guys were already half loaded.

"Nice." One guy slurred as his cronies laughed.

Valen tried to ignore him.

"Hey babe. Why not try a real man," another guy slurred.

Valen's patience was coming to an end. Finally, they reached the bartender.

"Seen, Samuel?" Valen asked.

"Yea, he was here not too long ago. May still be here. I dunno'."

"Thanks."

Valen turned to Rhiannon. "Samuel may still be here."

"Good. Let's find him and leave. I don't like this place, Valen."

"I know, and I'm beginning to regret that I brought you in."

As they turned to leave, what Valen was praying for not to happen, happened. A man stood and stopped them half way to the door.

"Nice lady ya' got there," he swayed.

"I heard you the first time," Valen said sharply. "Now if you'd excuse us, we were just leaving."

"Na, don't think so," the man slurred. "Not with her you ain't."

"Look. Stop trying to impress your friends," Valen said glaring at the guy's cronies. "We don't want any trouble. We just want to go."

As Valen continued to walk forward the guy pushed him back. "And I said you ain't."

Without thinking, Valen let go of Rhiannon's hand and lunged forward. His fist hit the man's chin hard and knocked him out cold.

Realizing what he did, he turned for Rhiannon. "I'm sorry, let's go."

Suddenly, the men from the table stood up. "You're not goin' nowhere, punk. You're gonna answer for our friend.

Valen knew exactly what he started. These guys loved to find reasons to fight, and Valen gave them the perfect one.

"The man said he was leaving and that's what you're gonna let him do," a voice from the back echoed.

In the shadows, Valen could make out a familiar figure.

"If you don't, you're all working overtime without pay. You got it!" The voice shouted. In the light Valen could see it was Samuel.

He was clean-shaven and neatly dressed. He was a sight for sore eyes.

The men at the table moaned, picked up their friend and left.

"Amazing," Valen smiled extending his hand. "I've never been happier to see you, Sam."

Their handshake turned to an embrace. "How ya' been," Valen continued.

"I've been good. Thanks for calling," Sam smiled smartly.

"Now, Sam. You know how I am with that stuff, but if it's worth anything, I am sorry."

"Don't worry about it. I did get your letters and assortment of pictures and prose. They were very good - as always. It's so good to see you, my friend, and I see you brought company," Samuel said bowing theatrically.

"Sam, meet Rhiannon. My wife."

"Well, hot dog! It's a pleasure to meet you, Rhiannon. I feel as though somehow I already know you," he said reaching to give her a hug.

"Same here, and thanks for the help," she smiled.

"So, when did all this happen?" Sam continued modestly.

"Few days ago," Valen said. "Just like I told you I hoped it would."

Sam turned to Rhiannon. "Yes m'am, this guy here, used to talk about you all the time. I sure am glad you wanted him. God knows no one else would," he laughed.

"So, Sam, what was that action all about just now?" Valen said gesturing toward the men that left.

"Well, you remember the money you left me before you flew out? Which by the way, I greatly appreciate," Sam nodded.

Valen just smiled modestly. He had left Sam a significant check before he left. He knew Sam wouldn't have taken it from him personally. So, he left it for him, knowing Imaginations would have never been possible without his help. He also knew he was going to need funds to keep everything running.

"How could I forget," Valen smiled.

"Well, I bought the loading docks and various other places throughout this whole town. If anything, to keep them from closing down and causing this place to be a ghost town. As a result, I've practically doubled the money already," he said modestly.

"That's great, Sam! Are you still working with those guys who bought our company?"

"No, we're completely out of it now. Actually, it only lasted a few months after you left and granted me authority to run things. It was quickly made obvious, they thought they knew how to do things better. And, frankly, it wasn't the same without you. Anyways, they amended our contract and so, I decided to start my own business."

"That's great! Your Aunt would be proud," Valen patted Sam's shoulder.

"Hope so," he smiled.

Rhiannon reached up and gave him a hug. "Congratulations, Sam. I feel as though we're all family."

"We are," Valen said. "So, now to the important stuff - where's my bike?"

"I took good care of her, don't you worry. That piece of rust is at my house. Come on, let's go," Sam teased.

"Hey, watch it," Valen smiled. "She may be a rust can , but that old piece of tin holds a lot of fond memories.

Valen and Rhiannon followed behind Samuel's oversized GMC to a rod iron gate. Samuel hung out the window, punched in a few codes and continued up the drive. One of the most beautiful homes Rhiannon, or Valen had ever seen sat atop acres of green rolling fields. Immaculate landscaping surrounded the home, adding to its elegance. It was a nontraditional replica of the classic southern estate. It had huge white columns, a grand porch and was decorated in intricate detail inside and out. Two arching staircases covered in scarlet carpet, connected the first and second floors. It was like a vision from the movies.

Samuel sat back quietly and just watched their expressions.

"So, do you like it?"

"Like it? It's incredible. We love it!" Valen cheered.

"It's beautiful," Rhiannon agreed.

"Well, make yourselves at home. What's mine is yours. By the way, is anyone hungry?"

"I'm starved," Rhiannon said.

"Come on. I'll fix us something to eat."

The kitchen was even more beautiful than the rest of the home. A huge brick oven was the first thing to catch Valen's eye. Then, it was the antique wood floors. The whole kitchen smelled delicious. It satisfied all the senses. Stainless steel appliances filled the workspace, colored tiles decorated the counters and a huge bay window provided most of the light during the day.

"How's turkey sandwiches sound?"

"Sounds good to me," Rhiannon smiled.

"Here, I'll help," Valen said reaching for the bread.

Samuel reached in the 'fridge and pulled out a few beers.

"Thanks, but none for me," Valen smiled. "I'll take some lemonade if you got it, though?"

"That sounds good - same for me," Rhiannon smiled.

"Well, that does sound good," Sam agreed. "Three lemonades coming up!"

"So, what made you decide to buy as much as you did, especially the docking business?" Valen asked.

"Well, as you know, I don't know much except how to drink and unload docks. So, with the card business losing its luster, I decided to buy Roy Thomson out."

Valen elaborated about Roy to Rhiannon.

"Roy was an older fisherman that looked as worn in years as his dog, Butch, did mangled. Butch was a shaggy old mutt that was missing one leg. He lost it after catching an infection from a rusty fishhook. Teeth protruded from Butch's mouth and his hair was thinning and tangled. He was truly the ugliest dog you ever saw. Together, Butch and Roy looked like a pitiful homeless pair, but in reality, Roy was a millionaire a thousand times over. He never married, but preferred instead to date young barmaids. It was rumored that several children in the town were his, but nothing was ever confirmed. He was a filthy and dirty-mouthed old man that cared for little in life other than money. He started his shipping company out of boredom, after years of service in the Navy. Eventually, due to lots of luck and timing, Roy's business grew from one ship to four."

"Anyway," Sam continued. "I approached Roy just before his death. He looked bad, but as you mentioned, he always looked bad. Surprisingly, Roy took my first offer and without a haggle. I already knew how to run the business from years of experience, and it just grew from there. I later bought several of the other stores in town. Now, the money rolls in. All it took was for someone to care and add some leadership. Nice ain't it?" Sam smiled big.

"Leadership definitely matters," Valen smiled.

Rhiannon caught Samuel up on what happened in Europe, and before anyone knew it, the sun was rising.

"Can you believe it? It's morning already?" Samuel said.

"Six a.m." Rhiannon yawned.

"Well, guys. I reckon' we ought to get some sleep. Your room's the first door on the right."

"It was nice catching up with you, Sam." Valen smiled.

"You too. Goodnight, y'all, or should I say good day."

With the sun shining bright through the windows, neither Rhiannon, Valen or Samuel could sleep that well. So, after only four hours, they found themselves back in the kitchen.

Valen and Sam, both being ones to take quick showers, were the first back downstairs.

"How'd ya' sleep," Sam asked.

"Not too good, but I don't care. It's been good seeing you again

187

ole' buddy."

"Yea, it is. So, where are you two going to live?"

"I don't know yet. We plan on looking soon though. We're ready to find a real home."

"I know what you mean," Sam smiled.

"You've done well for yourself, Sam. I'm glad to see it."

"Yea. Well, so did you, and I owe all of my success to you," Sam smiled.

"No, you don't. You got this all on your own," Valen confirmed.

Sam nodded proudly. "So, what are you gonna do now, Valen. It looks like all your dreams have come true."

"They have, Sam and to tell you the truth, I don't know what I'm going to do. And the funny thing is, I don't care. I feel like I've already accomplished everything I set out for."

"That's true, but a man's gotta have a passion, something to work for," Sam said edgingly, sensing there was something more Valen wanted to say.

"My passion is family now. And I don't want to fail at that. I never saw how a proper family is done, as you know. So, this is uncharted water for me. A true adventure to say the least. "

Valen nervously coughed to clear his throat. "I also know, I will never be the man, husband and father I desire to be without Jesus." Valen looked hesitantly up to see Sam's reaction. He wasn't going to let this opportunity pass by like last time.

Sam opened his eyes a bit surprised. "Jesus?"

"I know this may sound kinda' odd coming from me – your former drinking buddy, but I was running when we first met Sam, and in a way, I'm thankful, because my running led me to meet you. But, I'm not running from the truth I know anymore, and don't ever want to again. I was obsessed with money, again, as you know, and I thought that would bring me happiness. But strangely, it didn't. Then, I thought finding Rhiannon would bring me the happiness I was searching for – and she does. But, Sam, there's more to life. There's more to it than just getting. There's giving - but nothing I have to give is worth anything if not givin' in love, and it's difficult to love beyond myself, without Christ. My friend, Sherman tried to teach me this once, but I guess I have to learn things the hard way. Anyway, I just want to share this with you. We never talked much about our faith, and before I left, I wanted to share mine with you. You've done well, but I want you to know there's so much more, and I want you to know it – like I now know it."

Sam just sat there, silent. He had no idea what to say, but knew Valen was deathly serious. He could see the tears in his eyes and hear the love in his voice.

Just then, Rhiannon entered the room. Her hair still slightly wet from her shower. "I thought I heard my name. You guys talking about me behind my back?"

"Always," Valen smiled.

Valen quickly changed the subject. "Well, Sam, Rhiannon and I will probably be off this morning. We gotta' find that house, but I want us to stay in better touch. I will do a better job of that - you mean a lot to me."

"Well, you guys are welcome anytime, and I expect a phone call when you get settled. I want to be the first person to see your new home," Sam said extending his hand.

"Deal," Valen said returning the gesture. "So, let's see what kind of damage my bike's in."

Samuel led them to the garage and inside was Valen's bike shining like new. The engine had been completely replaced and a coat hanger no longer kept the exhaust in place. All the chrome was polished and the framework was without a scratch or a dent.

A hitch was attached to the bike, with all their luggage already loaded up.

"Sam, I don't believe you did this. I don't even recognize her."

"Good. She was lookin' rough."

Rhiannon stood off in the back and watched as Valen glowed like a schoolboy. "Thanks, Sam," he said wrapping his arms around his neck. "You're the best."

"I know. Now, you two get out of here, before I get choked up."

Sam turned to Rhiannon and met her embrace.

"Take care of him. He loves you more than life."

"I will, and thanks again, Sam."

Valen already on the bike threw the rental car keys to Samuel. "Could you return our car back?"

"I live for nothing else. I'm sure this minivan will do wonders for my image."

Rhiannon took her old spot on the back of Valen's bike and wrapped her arms around his waist.

"Thanks, Sam! Take care of yourself, and I'll talk to you soon," Valen shouted over the engine as they slowly made their way out of the garage.

"Good luck, guys!" Sam shouted waving goodbye.

Rhiannon turned and waved back as they drove down the long driveway. She was impressed, but despite his warm smile, sense of humor and success, something in his eyes reflected sadness. Something about him just seemed empty, as he stood alone in that big house. She tried to envision what it was like for both he and Valen years earlier. She had missed all of it, but was thankful for being with Valen now. For she too had once known that kind of loneliness. Now, her heart overflowed with gratitude for God leading them back together, and for the first time in her life, she was allowing herself to see His miracles.

As they drove away, Sam considered all Valen had shared with him. He was shocked at first, but as Valen was speaking, something inside was tugging at him. He knew Valen spoke the truth, and he was struggling with restlessness. A restlessness Valen knew all too well. At that moment, Sam realized he had been running from God as well, and he knew it was time to stop. He prayed to God and broke down in tears, falling to his knees, right there in the driveway.

From that day forward, Sam took a leap of faith and became a committed man to growing in his new faith. He had renewed purpose and his businesses became a platform where he was able to serve and share his faith in love with other restless souls like he once was.

Chapter XVII

They drove for miles all across the Southeast, staying at various hotels along the way. Although they could have lived anywhere, the South was home.

After touring most the Carolinas, parts of Tennessee and Alabama, Rhiannon and Valen settled in a small town in their home state of Georgia nestled along the banks of the Savannah River. Rolling pastures blanketed the landscape and giant pines reached into the deep blue sky. The particular property that caught their eye was a ranch-style home sitting atop 82 acres of this lush land. The site was truly breathtaking. It had a stable out to the side, and with barely a nudge, Rhiannon convinced the new owner to sell the horses already there. Valen paid the full asking price to include the horses, and for the first time in their lives, they felt at home.

The man they bought it from had recently inherited the land from his parents and was anxious to pocket the money. He was born and raised in that small town, but was now eager to make his way in the big city. Valen recognized the fiery ambition in his eyes immediately. For he had once shared it. He only hoped this young man, wouldn't burn himself up in the process of chasing his dreams, as he almost had.

Many who grow up in small towns can't wait to get out. However, in time, there's something about one's roots that can call you back. This was definitely true for Rhiannon and Valen. However, for now, this was definitely not the case for this young man. He wanted out and was set on staying out. Valen wished he could sit and pass along some wise counsel, but concluded it wasn't his place. Instead, he let the young man tell of all the big plans and dreams he was determined to accomplish.

After signing all the necessary papers, the house was theirs. The home was practically complete - a few personal touches were all that was needed. Rhiannon began immediately.

She had come to terms with the death of her family and was now excited about starting her own. Her entire life seemed to have been building up for this moment.

Valen was equally as excited. His first goal however was to ride the horses. There were three total, all varying in color and appearing in good health, although slightly slim. Jeb was a jet-black stallion and was the oldest and slower of the bunch. Coal, was a colorful mixture of red, brown and white and displayed the most energy. Then there was Gravity, the only female, young and vibrant. She was Valen's favorite. Gravity was full of personality and shined with a silky coat of golden brown. Her mane was long and flowing and when in full stride, she looked like an angel gliding on the wind. Gravity took to Valen immediately as well and followed him endlessly as he introduced himself to the rest of the property.

Rhiannon watched in amusement as Valen played and chased the horses as if they were puppies.

"I see you've made some friends," she smiled.

"They're beautiful aren't they?" Valen said gazing in amazement as the horses ran across the field.

"Incredible," Rhiannon agreed. "So, when are you going to let me ride 'em?"

"How 'bout now?"

Valen led Rhiannon to the stable where the saddles were kept. The horses quickly followed. Anxious to have someone ride them again, they took their positions as if on cue.

Rhiannon had learned a lot about horses and how to ride from her Dad. Rhiannon's father had been raised on a farm and owned a horse all his life. When Rhiannon was young, he bought her a horse named, Sadie. Sadie was majestic and looked as if she belonged in a royal procession. She was bleach white and full of grace. Whenever Rhiannon rode her, Sadie would stride gently to comfort any fears Rhiannon may have had. They were friends, and her father would often wake early to find his daughter riding in the morning's dew.

Rhiannon and her dad rode several days a week and bonded in the silence and tranquility of nature. Seeing these horses brought a wave of memories back to Rhiannon's heart. The hardest day in the world was when her father died. After that, Rhiannon couldn't bear to ride alone. It was simply too hard. So, as a result, her mother sold Sadie. It was a day Rhiannon always regretted. Seeing Sadie hauled away by new owners was unbearable, and a deep sorrow she would occasionally relive in her dreams.

Now, with Valen's smile and excitement with the horses, Rhiannon felt reattached to the fond memories of her past. She could ride again and have someone to enjoy it with. It was a good day.

Rhiannon showed Valen the basics of hitching a saddle and the proper riding posture. He had trouble with the flow at first, but was quick to get the hang of it and was soon riding Gravity at full stride.

Rhiannon rode Coal and immediately became fond of his energy. He was feisty and independent, but at the same time, kind and gentle. Rhiannon thought how beautiful he was and how fluid and perfect he rode. A sparkle returned to Coal's eyes. He was happy to be ridden again.

Jeb, too old to ride, would watch and run beside Valen and Rhiannon as they rode. He tired quickly, but still tried to keep up. He was a beautiful horse and would often poke his nose into Valen and Rhiannon as if asking to be ridden. They would oblige at times, but within minutes, Jeb would start wheezing and hanging his head in exhaustion.

The five of them became a family, and the horses were happy to have the attention again. Their previous owners, the Dusts, had bought them all at once at an auction years earlier and used to ride them constantly. They bought three just in case their son, John, ever wanted to ride, but he never did. Eventually, the Dusts got too old to ride, and their attention turned to the caring of one another's health. The horses eventually grew slightly withdrawn from neglect.

Valen and Rhiannon's love and attention renewed their previous kinship to people and seemed to literally bring them back to life.

Each horse had a unique personality and although they looked as figures of strength, they were actually quite sensitive. Rhiannon was aware of their previous neglect and perhaps due to some past guilt, she awoke early every morning to brush and ride them in the morning mist, just like she had done as a girl.

"You know, we're probably going to need a truck, or something to haul things around out here. I don't think my motorcycle is going to cut it," Valen smiled one morning as they brushed the horses. "If we need to take these guys into town, or simply drive around, a truck sure would come in handy."

"That'd be great." Rhiannon agreed. "You know, I haven't driven in years?" Being that I lived in the city, I took taxis wherever I had to go. I would love to have a truck, but it has to be baby blue."

"Let's do it then. Come on," Valen said reaching for Rhiannon's hand.

On the back of Valen's bike, Rhiannon leaned over to speak in his ear. "I can't believe all this is happening. It's too fantastic, Valen. My life is truly blessed. Thank you."

"No, thank you," Valen said.

At the car lot, Rhiannon saw the exact truck she wanted, and after a test drive, it was a done deal. The exterior was baby blue with tan leather interior. The inside was filled with every electronic gadget one could think of. The truck was only a truck in body style everything else was luxury. Rhiannon was like a little schoolgirl and looked like one behind the wheel. Valen laughed to himself as he followed Rhiannon home on his bike. Who would've thought a lady that looked as elegant as her wouldn't want a pickup. Her tom-boyish nature made Valen smile.

After a few weeks in their new place, most of the redecorating was complete, and their house was made a home. In addition, they bought new dishes, pots, pans, silverware and glasses. It was the first time for either of them that they had needed such things. They were much older now and laughed at how neither of them had ever had to pick out silverware before. Most of what they had had been hand-me-downs, or in Valen's case, plastic plates and utensils.

More dreams than they could've possibly imagined were coming true, and they felt truly blessed. However, an unspoken desire to have children occupied both their minds.

At an earlier age, Rhiannon was told by her doctor that it may be difficult for her later in life to conceive children. Rhiannon and her mother declined to have a procedure done that might have provided some help. At the time, it wasn't a major concern for Rhiannon, but today, the thought of not being able have children with Valen was haunting. She wanted to make a family more than words could express, and she prayed God would allow it.

It was this concern that led her to pick up the Bible they had been given at their wedding by the Peacocks. She found comfort and assurance in it and in time, discovered a peace deep within her that as she trusted God with her life, she could trust any outcome to be used for good. As result, her spirit moved from fear to faith.

Valen was initially aware something was wrong, because every time he mentioned kids, or saw Rhiannon around children, she would become teary-eyed. So, he mostly left the subject alone and allowed her to share her feelings when she felt comfortable.

Early one morning, Rhiannon and Valen, keeping with their early morning tradition of riding Coal and Gravity, went out to the river that flowed through their land to watch the sun's ascent. As always, older Jeb followed.

"It never ceases to amaze me how beautiful this place is," Valen said.

"I know, it reminds me of a poem I once read," said Rhiannon. "I think it went something like...'I don't think I'll ever see a poem as lovely as a tree. For God makes a tree, and poems are made from men like me.' I only wish I could remember who wrote it."

"Wordsworth." Valen stated.

Rhiannon pushed Valen on the arm as to knock him over, "Know it all," she smiled.

"Hey," he continued. "What do you think about getting some more animals around here, like maybe a dog and cat?"

Rhiannon just nodded and shrugged as if asking why not.

"Yea, I think it would be nice. What do you think?" He asked again for verbal confirmation.

"Sounds good," Rhiannon smiled.

"Ok - It will be nice. I know we don't have any kids yet and..."

"Speaking of that," Rhiannon interrupted. "I need to tell you something."

Valen prepared himself. "What?" he said as nonchalantly as possible.

"When I was younger, I was told I have a condition that may make it difficult to have children," Rhiannon said straining confidence.

Valen remained silent.

"Valen, I'm sorry I'm just telling you this. I know it probably wasn't fair, but I was afraid."

"Afraid of what Rhiannon? That I wouldn't love you, or want you? Rhiannon, you know better," he said softly.

Valen climbed down from Gravity and walked toward Rhiannon.

"Come here," he said reaching to help her down.

"I love you, no matter what. You know that." Valen gently placed his hand under her chin and raised her head. "I love you," he repeated.

Rhiannon fell into Valen's arms and cried. "I'm sorry, Valen. I'm sorry."

"Don't be. I promise, whatever happens, don't be sorry. It's not your fault. Besides, it's still possible for us to have kids, and if it proves not to be, adoption is always an option. So, please, don't cry."

"I love you." Rhiannon squeezed him tight. "I love you so much." Rhiannon looked up into his eyes. "I thank God for you in my prayers, Valen, every day."

Valen held Rhiannon and looked to the sky. He thanked God for her too. He thanked God for his life, and he prayed for strength to always be able to protect her and to deal with whatever the future would bring.

"Now, com'on. Let's go get a dog," Valen edged, as he helped her back on Coal.

"Sounds good," she said wiping the tears from her eyes.

Their first stop was the humane society. It always broke Valen's heart to see the animals locked up, but knew it was better for them to be there than wandering the streets with nothing to eat and potentially being struck by a car.

As Valen and Rhiannon looked into each cage, he could almost read the animals expressions. In some, he could see fear, anger, sorrow and pain. In others, their eyes and body language expressed joy, excitement and eagerness. Each was so different. It was hard to pass some over. They were looking for a Golden Retriever type and knew they weren't likely to find a full breed at the kennel, but they still wanted to look there first.

One tiny female puppy stood out from all the rest. She resembled a retriever, but clearly had some other bloodline. Rhiannon thought it was probably Chow. The puppy was very affectionate and independent. She had an attitude and personality Rhiannon and Valen fell in love with immediately. She had large feet, indicating she would most likely grow to be a big dog and had a long thick coat. She was beautiful. Realizing she was the one, Rhiannon nodded to Valen as the puppy lay lazily in her arms.

"What about this one?" she asked cautiously.

"It doesn't matter to me, hon'. She looks like a good one," he smiled petting the puppies ears. "Besides, I like knowing we can give her a nice home compared to where she started."

"Let's do it then," Rhiannon smiled as the puppy licked her face. "Let's take her home."

After signing all the papers, shots were given and an appointment was made to have her spayed.

"What if we want her to have puppies?" Rhiannon asked the assistant at the desk.

"Sorry, ma'm. All animals from this society must be fixed. It's a safety measure, for the animals' sake. We don't want more to end up without homes."

"I understand," Rhiannon sighed. "Oh well, we better have those kids to keep her company then," she said nudging Valen.

Valen opened the door to the truck for Rhiannon and helped her in. "So, what are we going to name her?" he asked.

"Abby," she said. "I think she looks like an Abby."

"Then, Abby it is," Valen said patting the puppy's head. "She's definitely a cutie."

By the time Valen and Rhiannon made it home, the sun was starting to set, and an orange glow painted everything in its dim light. Rhiannon could hardly wait to play with the puppy and quickly darted out of the car and into the front living room with Abby in her arms.

The room had been newly renovated with solid oak flooring, was decorated in a Southwestern style. Miniature statues of Indians and cowboys rustling horses sat upon the tabletops, and a slight scent of cinnamon apple potpourri filled the air. The couch was large and spacious and accented the room's cozy nature with its dark khaki color. An antique chest served as their coffee table, and an old brick fireplace stained with marshmallow droppings and soot, waited to warm the winter's frost. Nowhere in the room was a TV. Instead, books of varying sorts filled the walls. Although some went unread, most were enjoyed spontaneously from time-to-time.

Rhiannon plopped on the couch with Abby and began playing a gentle game of tug-of-war with one of her old bandannas. Valen sat on the chair beside them and smiled as he watched.

He was surprised it had taken Rhiannon so long to talk to him about her condition, but he was pleased she finally did. Deep down, he felt sad about the whole thing and prayed that they would be able to have children. Rhiannon would be such a good mother, and he wanted the chance to be the father he never had.

That night, Valen decided to put the whole issue out of his head and to trust the situation to God. He had been spending most of his early morning rides reading the Bible he found months earlier tucked away in an old saddle bag hanging in the barn. It was worn, written in, underlined and highlighted throughout. It was also inscribed on the inside, "To my dearest - I love you." It apparently had been given from the wife of the former owner to her husband.

What began first as a curious exploration of the notes written along the margins and a summarization of the highlighted verses had now become a growing exploration for truth and a deepening desire to know God's word.

Each morning as the sun rose, Valen was rediscovering the faith he had been introduced to so long ago and blindly running from for far too long. His seemingly lifelong restlessness was finally being replaced with a deep inner rest.

That night, Rhiannon laid sleeping soundly beside him, and the puppy sat at the foot of the bed. It was a beautiful family, and he smiled as he leaned over to kiss Rhiannon. "I love you," he whispered as he gazed at the blessing beside him. She was beautiful as her hair laid wildly across her pillow. To Valen, she was like a dream. The years had passed so fast and so much had happened that he couldn't believe this was all true. So tonight, as he did many nights, Valen lay quietly in the warmth of his home and took it all in.

Overcome with emotion, he gently kissed her neck. Rhiannon woke to meet him with an embrace. Neither said a word, but held each other tightly.

The next morning, they were woken by the puppy's wet kiss. Valen was first to be attacked and then Rhiannon. Valen pulled Abby to him and rubbed her ears. Rhiannon rolled over to rest on Valen's shoulder.

Valen laid his hand on Rhiannon's back and scratched it softly.

"So, what project are we going to hit today?" He asked.

Rhiannon untangled the necklace around her neck and simply shrugged.

"I know," Valen said coyly. "Let's make those final changes to the house we've been talking about."

"What? Painting?" Rhiannon sighed.

"Yeah. Painting, polishing, some gardening - all of it."

"Well, if we're going to do all that, then we best get started,"

Rhiannon said sarcastically.

She actually loved doing all that stuff, but she also loved complaining about it.

Both of them got dressed without a shower and immediately took their positions. They knew what had to be done and knew what their jobs were. Around the house was a picket fence, speckled with white flaking paint. Valen began the process of sanding and repainting the fence to its original splendor.

Rhiannon attended to the overgrowth in front of and behind the house. Flowers and bushes of all sorts outlined the home, but had gone un-manicured for some time. Rhiannon and Valen both met their duties in full force and worked arduously under the summer's hot sun.

The other jobs that needed attending to included repainting and repairing various parts of the stable, as well as repainting the home's shutters and some of its rooms. Weeks past and soon the fence, landscaping, barn and barn shutters were back to their glorious charm.

However, just before finishing the house shutters, the last detail to be addressed, Rhiannon fell dizzy from a ladder. She hit the ground hard and lost her breath on impact. When she finally managed a gasp, she screamed for Valen on the other side of the house.

"What happened? Are you okay?" He shouted, seeing Rhiannon on the ground.

"Yes," she wheezed, still struggling for air. "But for some reason, I just got dizzy, lost my balance and fell."

"I can see that. Come on," Valen leaned to help Rhiannon up.
"Let's go lay down for a while inside."

Fall was quickly approaching, so the heat wasn't as bad as it had
been weeks before, but Valen still thought it was the temperature
that got to her.

"I'm sure it's the heat. You'll be okay. Do you want some water?"

Rhiannon nodded.

As Valen left the room, Rhiannon touched her stomach. Her
instincts told her it was something more than the weather.

"Here," Valen said handing her a glass. "I bet you got shaken up
out there?" he smiled.

Rhiannon glared back.

"Now, don't get mad. I know what it's like to get the wind
knocked out of you. It scares me when it happens. What do you
say we call it quits for the day and turn on some music instead."
Valen walked over to turn on the stereo where he selected to play
their favorite variety of jazz.

As days past, Rhiannon's symptoms grew worse. She got head
spins more often and felt wheezy whenever she ate. One evening
as Valen stood in the kitchen making his homemade pizza,
Rhiannon sat on the counter beside him eating cereal. Anytime
Valen cooked they would always talk about their day, as he
crafted his self-proclaimed masterpieces. "You're gonna' ruin
your appetite," he smiled as she crunched down on her cereal. "I
don't know why you do that?"

206

"What?" Rhiannon mumbled with a mouthful.

"Eat just before we're getting ready to eat? You waste your appetite, just before the good stuff is ready."

Rhiannon smiled and shrugged innocently.

As Valen pulled the pizza from the oven, Rhiannon suddenly buckled-over in pain.

"What's wrong?" Valen said rushing to her.

"Nothing, just these stomach cramps I've been getting lately. Valen, I'm worried. Something's not right. I know my body, and I'm telling you, something's not right."

"Okay, do you want to go to the emergency room?"

"Not yet. Maybe if they don't go away soon. Besides, I have to have some of your world famous pizza," Rhiannon grimaced, straining to smile.

Valen knew Rhiannon was strong and didn't like to look weak, but these symptoms were worrying him. The next morning, Rhiannon was back to her old self and didn't feel the need to go to the doctor.

"I'm fine, Valen, honestly. There's really no need."

"Com'on, quit being a baby. Just last night, you were buckled over in pain."

"Yes, I know, but now I'm fine."

Valen grabbed Rhiannon's hand and headed for the door. "It's better to know for sure."

Valen and Rhiannon waited in the doctor's office for about half-an-hour, when they were finally called to the back and waited another twenty minutes there. Finally, the doctor came in.

"Mr. and Mrs. McCloud, my name's, Dr. Daniel Jones," he said extending his hand to Valen first.

"Nice to meet you doctor. And please, call us Valen and Rhiannon."

"Okay, and please, call me Daniel. We all know I'm a doctor, there's no need to advertise it," he smiled. "So, what seems to be the trouble?"

"Well, nothing at the moment," Rhiannon said. "But sometimes I get these awful stomach cramps and dizzy spells."

"I see," Daniel said adjusting his stethoscope to his ears. "Breath deep for me."

Dr. Jones was a slender gentleman with a classic southern accent. He spoke as if he were royalty, but maintained a manner that was open and approachable. His head was bald, outlined with thinning hair, and by the thickness of his glasses it was safe to assume his eyesight was past bad. Daniel was a self-professed addict of fishing and his skin was like tanned leather from his hours spent on the water. He was definitely a joyful person and had a dry, sarcastic humor. He and Rhiannon got along instantly.

Valen sat in the chair at the edge of the small room and watched. Rhiannon met his glance and rolled her eyes in an expression of assurance that she was fine.

Daniel took some blood and performed other routine procedures. "If you two will excuse me, I'm going to check on the blood work," he said. "I'll be right back."

"Well, he certainly is being thorough," Valen said.

"Yes, I know. I hope he doesn't find anything wrong."

"I'm sure it will all be okay."

"Rhiannon?" Daniel said walking back into the room. "If you don't mind, I'd like to conduct a pregnancy test while we have your blood work as well. That okay with you? It could definitely explain your symptoms."

"Really?" Valen smiled. Rhiannon sat silent.

"Sure," Rhiannon said hesitantly.

"Okay, I'll be right back," the doctor smiled.

Valen nodded.

"Honey, this is great! You might be pregnant!"

"Don't get too excited Valen, I'm trying not to."

After some time had passed, the doctor knocked on the door.

"Come in," both Rhiannon and Valen said with bated breath.

"Well folks, I'm proud to announce that you two are definitely going to have a baby."

"Yes!" Valen shouted as he reached for Rhiannon.

"You did it honey! You're gonna be a mommy!" He said kissing her forehead.

Rhiannon sat crying with joy.

"Congratulations," Daniel said patting both of their shoulders. "Now, go home," he smiled. "I'll see you soon."

Neither Valen nor Rhiannon said a word on the drive home. Instead, both sat quietly smiling - alone with their thoughts.

As they drove up the driveway with gravel grinding beneath their wheels, they were immediately greeted by a tail wagging Abby.

"Hey girl," Valen said climbing from the truck. Rhiannon sat motionless. "Honey? You coming in?" As if waking from a daze, Rhiannon nodded.

"Sorry. I guess I never expected this day to come. I just can't stop thinking about it."

"Me either, hon'," Valen said hugging her. "It's a dream come true."

Morning sickness came quick for Rhiannon, and Valen was relentless in his pampering of her. Rhiannon was one that hated being dependent on someone else and was quick to irritabilities. However, Valen stood strong with his patience and love and often laughed quietly to himself, thankful for the blessing that was developing in her belly.

"You know Rhiannon, I was thinking. I've always wanted to play the guitar, and I think now's the best time. I can serenade you and our baby. Besides, I hear music is good for growing babies."

"Whatever you think," Rhiannon said through a forced smile.

"Yea, and you can play with me," Valen teased.

As part of her mother's focus on raising Rhiannon with proper etiquette, she was taught to play the piano at an early age and became quite good. However, she hadn't played in years. It resurrected memories of her mother sitting beside her during lessons. Besides, she hadn't been in the presence of a piano since she left home.

"Sure, I'll play with you," Rhiannon smiled. "But you're forgetting one major factor."

"What's that?"

"A piano and a guitar," Rhiannon smiled.

Valen laughed. "Yea, looks like I got ahead of myself again."

"So..." Valen said changing the subject, "how are you feeling?"

"Fine, I'm a little queasy, but it's nothing a little ice cream wouldn't fix."

"Honey, you've already gone through two pints. How could you possibly want more?"

"I don't know. Chocolate mint must be the baby's favorite."

"I'll be right back," Valen grinned.

Valen was gone for some time, and Rhiannon was beginning to worry. Rising from the couch, she walked to the living room window and looked outside. The truck was gone and the sky was turning gray. Rhiannon closed the blinds and turned on the radio for the weather report. Wondering where Valen went, she peered out the kitchen window again, poured her some milk and returned to the couch to await his return.

She soon heard the sound of tires on gravel and Abby's bark. As the front door opened, a wave of relief flooded through her, but soon turned to anger. "Where did you go?" She demanded, but as she turned she saw Valen standing there innocently with a gallon of ice cream in one hand and a new guitar in the other.

Surprised, she smiled and changed her tone, "You could have at least called."

"Yea, but then it wouldn't have been a surprise."

"So, you're really going to learn how to play that thing?"

"Absolutely - I have a captured audience right here," he smiled.

Valen made Rhiannon her traditional three-scoop bowl of ice cream and sat down with his new guitar and lesson book to begin practicing.

Rhiannon read her magazines and did her best to ignore the painful plucking that echoed from the back room.

Hours past, and with Rhiannon's encouragement, Valen had given up practicing for the night. The rain outside was pouring, and Valen and Rhiannon cuddled by the fire. Rhiannon rubbed Valen's hand and stared at his naked finger. "I have to get you a ring on that finger. I can't believe we haven't done that yet."

"It's not a big deal. Your engagement ring is the most symbolic to me."

"I know," Rhiannon smiled. "I just want everyone to know that you're taken and belong to me."

"They can tell it by that leash you keep around my neck," Valen laughed.

Rhiannon jumped on his stomach and playfully pinned him to the ground. "You take that back," she smiled.

Valen was just about to give in when they were startled by the doorbell's ring.

"Who could that be in this weather?" Rhiannon questioned.

Valen was silent, doing his best to hide a smile. "You got me," he said standing. "Let's go see."

When they opened the door, four men stood soaking in the rain. "We have the delivery you requested, Mr. McCloud.

"Yes, thank you. Please, come on in out of the rain."

"What delivery?" Rhiannon asked peering over the couch like a child.

"Oh, just a little something I ordered when I went out earlier."

"Where would you like us to put it, sir?" The head delivery guy asked.

"In the corner of the sunroom. Follow me, I'll show you."

Rhiannon sat quietly with anticipation. Although she had a pretty good idea as to what it was.

Within minutes, the deliverymen had a brand new, black, baby-grand piano set up in their home. It was truly beautiful. The most beautiful piano Rhiannon had ever seen.

"Oh, Valen. I can't believe you did this? It's breathtaking."

"Well, I look forward to hearing you play, and personally, I can't wait to play with you...one day"

As Valen tipped the men generously, Rhiannon ran over to her new piano like a schoolgirl. She brushed her hand against its cold polished wood and admired its complex simplicity. Hesitantly and quietly, she began to play. She pressed the keys softly, producing a sound that almost whispered. Valen sat in the chair behind her and watched smiling. A damp Abby jumped into his lap.

Slowly, Rhiannon's confidence grew and her music amplified. Her body swayed with emotion as she closed her eyes to play her favorite piece, Chopin: Mazurka No. 4. Valen was entranced, wishing the moment would never end. He sat admiring her beauty, knowing she was truly gifted. Her belly was now slightly rounded and her body enveloped with the mysterious sweetness of pregnancy.

Rhiannon played for hours, as if the opportunity was her last. She was in another world - another time. And she played as if for heaven.

God had blessed them, and at that moment it was as if angels surrounded them. They danced all around. Purity, grace and innocence hung thick in the air. Paradise seemed to be truly theirs.

That night, both Rhiannon and Valen slept more soundly than ever before. Music danced in their minds and in their hearts, and their love grew stronger.

Chapter XVIII

Every morning before Rhiannon woke, Valen would tiptoe downstairs, start a pot of coffee and continue with his guitar practice. His determination was unyielding, and never once did he give into the frustration that learning to play the guitar can create. His fingers ached with anticipation and work, but became more skilled with each lesson.

It was the same as everything else in Valen's life - he had to work hard to get it. Although many would say he stumbled into success. He knew the hard work it took to get there, like years of confusion and grunt work at the docks. He was glad for those times though, for he knew that he wouldn't appreciate the things he had, if he hadn't worked so hard to obtain them.

With each passing month, Rhiannon's stomach grew larger with life, and Valen became a more accomplished guitarist. Their nights were filled with Valen making market runs for ice cream and periodic serenades from his guitar.

Rhiannon's moods bounced fiercely in every direction, and Valen did his best emotional juggling act, remaining always cautious for her moment of labor. Although Rhiannon tried to help with the cooking and cleaning, it was Valen that took on all the household duties.

"Valen, seriously, let me do something."

"No, now you know what the doctor said, and we're going to stick to it."

"Ah, doctors are always over cautious. They don't want to get sued," Rhiannon smiled, hobbling her way over to Valen, who was in the kitchen making his famous pizza again.

"Honey, what do you need? I told you to ask me, and I'll get it for you."

"I just want to sit in here and talk to you. Is that okay?" she said testily.

"Yes, I'm sorry. I don't mean to be a pest. I just want to make sure everything goes well," he said patting her belly.

"I know, and so do I, but I have to have a little bit of a normal life," Rhiannon smiled.

"You know, I'm glad we get to spend our days together. I amazingly never seem to tire of you," he chided.

"Ah, I'm sure I have to get on your nerves sometimes," Rhiannon said.

"Well, yeah, but to be with you during this whole thing is nice. You know?"

"Yes, it is," Rhiannon leaned over to kiss his cheek.

Valen noticed a tear coming from her eye. "Now, what in the world are you crying for?"

"I don't know, these darn hormones of mine are driving me crazy," she said busting out in tears.

Valen walked over to hold her. "You're crazy you know that," Valen smiled, as he wrapped his hands around her ears and kissed her forehead.

"You wanna' go see a movie tonight?" he asked.

"No, not really, let's eat that world famous pizza of yours and make a pallet on the floor instead,"

"No complaints from me. Now, get in there and let me wait on you hand and foot - you know it's what I live for," Valen smirked.

"Of course you do," Rhiannon said tossing her hair to one side and prancing off.

Next to the fire, Rhiannon made a pallet on the floor. Together, in the silence, warmed by the fire, they sat, ate and dreamed of what was to come.

"You know Christmas isn't too far off now?" Valen interrupted.

"Yes, I know."

"So, what do you want from Santa this year?"

"Nothing, I have all I could ever want here with you three," Rhiannon smiled petting Abby with one hand and her belly with the other.

"Yeah, I guess you're right, we are a handful. Oh, well, perhaps Santa will surprise you."

"Perhaps," Rhiannon smiled laying her head against his shoulder, "Perhaps."

Valen slept on the floor that night while Rhiannon captured the couch. They were woken by the sun's warm glow. Valen was the first to rise and start the morning coffee. Still in yesterday's clothes, he walked outside to enjoy the crisp morning air.

It was nearing winter, but the colors were still vibrant and magic. In the distance, the horses were running to greet Valen and get their breakfast of mixed grain. Valen laughed at how they acted so similar to overgrown puppies. "Morning, gang. How y'all feeling today?" Valen smiled scratching their chins and patting their rumps. "Com'on let's go get some food!"

Valen ran as if threatening a race, but the horses simply played at a gallop. Abby on the other hand, beat them all to the stable and barked cheerfully in victory.

When Valen returned to the house, the coffee was full, the pallet had been picked up and Rhiannon was in the shower.

Their shower was a large standing one with three separate shower heads - one located in the front, one behind and one in the lower middle. The entire shower was surrounded by glass. So, when Valen walked in, he could see Rhiannon shaded by rising steam. Somehow, her pregnant outline seemed more beautiful than any sight he had ever seen. Valen crept back out slowly so not to disturb her and closed the door behind him quietly.

Valen poured his coffee and began practicing his guitar once again - reflecting on the bounty of his life and wondering why God had poured such favor in recent years. Clearly, he didn't deserve it, and he wondered why him?

Weeks past, and it wasn't long before snow blanketed their home. This particular winter was colder than most, and so Valen and Rhiannon decided to install a small heating system in the stable to help keep the horses comfortable. It was an unnecessary purchase they were sure, but it helped them worry less to know old Jeb and the others wouldn't freeze to death during the harsh winter nights.

Rhiannon was showing significantly now. However, they still didn't know whether it was a girl or a boy; and they didn't want to know, until delivery.

Christmas was around the corner, and as always, Valen was in full holiday spirits. Fires burned in the fireplace most every night, and Christmas songs filled the house. Colored lights decorated the outside of their home and stable. Even though Valen preferred white lights, Rhiannon had always wanted colored. Her house growing up always had white and she always wanted colored. So, she decided early on that whenever she had a home, colored lights would rule.

Valen had Rhiannon's gift already selected. They had never bought each other the wedding bands they had promised and didn't feel rushed to do so, but this Christmas, Valen had the perfect one selected. It was surrounded completely with diamonds and would match her engagement ring perfectly. Ironically, Rhiannon had also selected Valen's ring. She felt it was time for him to show the world that he belonged to her. Both had them hidden in places they thought the other would never look.

A few days before the 25th, Valen had plans to launch his new family tradition of setting out into the woods with his horse and dog to find their Christmas tree, chopping it down, and dragging it home the old fashioned way.

Rhiannon was amused by his childish excitement and wished she could go with him.

"Hurry back home now, I don't want to wait for you too long."

"I will," Valen said kissing her stomach. "You and our baby just stay here bundled next to that fire."

"Com'on Abby!" Valen shouted. "You get to face the cold with me girl." Abby was now quite large and thick with hair, and although mostly grown, she was just an oversized puppy.

Outside, Valen hopped on Coal who was already saddled and bobbing her head with eagerness to go.

Approaching their home however, was a white Explorer. Valen noticed it as being new to the area and that the two teenagers inside appeared drunk. Valen waved and gestured for them to slow down, but the kids quickly turned their heads and continued on their way. Frustrated, Valen reluctantly continued toward his destination.

It didn't take long for him to find a tree that met his liking. It was cold and Valen wanted to get back to his warm house and be with his wife. So, he quickly began to chop the tree down, but with every chop, Abby was howling. In fact, she began to act wild, barking, scratched at the snow, whining and running in circles.

Back home, at the same moment, Rhiannon had decided to check the mail. She made her way carefully down the driveway to the mailbox. It was a long walk, but she felt the exercise and cold air in her lungs would do the baby well. Suddenly, as she sorted through the mail, the same truck Valen saw earlier came racing back down the street. Noticing Rhiannon on the curb, the kid driving made a sharp turn to avoid her. But the road was iced. He slid faster towards her. Rhiannon couldn't move. She saw the truck in slow motion approach her. But it was happening too fast. She couldn't react. The impact crashed her against a tree and knocked her unconscious.

Shocked the two boys staggered toward their victim. Splashes of blood stained the snow and envelopes were scattered around her.

"Nolan! I can't believe this. What do we do?" The young passenger cried.

Nolan stood silent in disbelief. He felt as if he were in a nightmare. Frightened by the sight of Rhiannon's twisted body, he panicked and ran back to the truck.

"Nolan! Where are you going? We have to do something!"

Nolan started the engine. "Get in, or I'm leaving you!"

The boy stared at Rhiannon, as she gasped for air. He debating what to do, but not wanting to take the blame alone, he climbed back in the truck. Together they sped off.

"Calm down, Abby! No! Down!" Abby scratched at Valen's legs. Shaking his head and dismissing the dog as crazy, Valen began tying the tree's trunk by rope to the horn of his saddle. "Okay girl, we can go now," and with that, Abby was gone.

Not wanting to damage the tree's limbs, Valen took it slow as the tree dragged from behind, but by the time he got home everything was in mass hysteria.

Abby was howling as he approached, and all of the horses were huffing and stamping wildly.

A coldness clamped Valen's soul and his hands went numb when he saw Rhiannon lying near the street. "Oh, my God," he screamed racing to her. "Rhiannon!"

The horror pierced Valen's heart and strangled his throat. Falling to his knees, he reached for his wife and held her in his arms. She was still breathing! Blood poured from her nose and covered her body. Her face was ghost white.

Without hesitation, Valen raced her to the car and rushed to the hospital. During the drive, Valen prayed to God and cried tears of fear for her survival.

Valen held firm to Rhiannon's hand. Blood, continued to drip from her wounds. She was fading fast.

Upon reaching the hospital, Valen pulled Rhiannon from the truck and burst into the emergency room. "Someone, please help me! Please! It's my wife!"

The emergency crew was quick to action and within minutes had Rhiannon hooked to a life support system. However, it was hours before Valen would see her again. Seconds passed like days. The waiting was excruciating. Accelerating emotions of anger, fear, loss and hope raced through him as he paced the halls. His mind was losing more control with each step.

Finally, a doctor came to him. "Mr. McCloud, your wife is a victim of a hit and run, and I have mixed news about her condition."

"Can I see her?"

"Well, first let me...."

"No!" Valen said grabbing the doctor's coat. "Can I see my wife?"

"Yes, sir, Room 2111."

Valen flew down the hall to Rhiannon's room, but stopped suddenly at the door. "Thank you, God," he said as he stepped slowly into the room.

Rhiannon was awake, but obviously weak and dazed with shock.

"Honey? Oh, God, please…" He cried kneeling by her side.

"Valen," she whispered.

"Yes, honey?"

"Do you know?"

"Know what, hon'?" Valen said cradling and kissing her hand.

"About the baby?"

Startled and shaken as if woken from a dream, Valen felt guilt for not even thinking about the baby. Before this moment, all his thoughts and concerns were for her.

"No, what about our baby?"

"We could lose him," Rhiannon cried. "It's a boy…the doctors told me," she clinched Valen's hand tighter.

Valen remained silent.

"And the doctors don't know if I'm going to pull out of this, Valen," Rhiannon continued.

"What? What are you talking about?" Valen laughed with disbelief.

"There was a lot of damage done and there's a good possibility I'm not going to make it," Rhiannon's eyes filled with tears.

"Nonsense, you're going to be fine, and we're going to have lots of children."

"No!" Rhiannon strained. "Listen to me, we have to save this baby," but soon after the words left her mouth, she passed out due to weakness.

"Rhiannon. Rhiannon! Talk to me."

"She can't hear you," a voice said from behind.

Valen didn't even turn to see who it was.

"She's tired and her body's stressed, Mr. McCloud. We need to talk."

Valen bowed his head in Rhiannon's hair and took a deep breath, then stood. "I know," he said.

"Let's step outside," the doctor frowned.

Valen followed into a private room and waited for the doctor to begin the conversation.

"I'm truly sorry to have to tell you this, but your wife is bleeding internally and we can't to anything more to help her."

Valen walked to the window and stood silent.

"However, we can save your baby. Remarkably, no damage has been done, but we must take action as soon as possible. Your wife is getting weak and your baby runs a risk of dying."

"I see," Valen said in a calm agitated voice. "And I'm supposed to choose between my wife and baby? Well, I'm sorry doctor, but I can't make that kind of choice!"

"No, you don't understand. You have no choice, your wife will most likely die due to internal bleeding. So, we can either save your son now, or run the risk of losing him too if we wait. I'm sorry to be so blunt, but we must act now."

"My wife is fine. I was just in there having a conversation with her!"

"Yes, and it's remarkable she even had the strength. Look, sir, all we need is your signature allowing us to perform a C - Section and to take your son to intensive care. We will leave your wife on life support as long as possible."

Valen stood silent.

"Sir, try to understand that we're losing valuable time concerning the life of your child."

"After the operation, will I be able to see my wife."

"If she survives past the operation, but I must be honest with you and say that it's highly unlikely."

"So, you need a decision now?"

"Yes, sir, we do."

Valen reached for the papers reluctantly and signed them. "Let me see my wife first, okay?" he said as tears ran down his face.

"Please hurry," urged the doctor.

Rhiannon was still unconscious when Valen walked into the room, but as soon as he touched her face, as if sensing his presence, she awoke. Her eyes were dim, but to Valen, she was still as beautiful as ever.

"Hey, hon'," he smiled.

"Hey," she smiled knowingly. "You're going to be a good father," she cried.

Valen couldn't speak, and tears once again, poured from his eyes.

"I know this is hard, but it's the only thing to do. A part of us lives on, and I want you to teach him all the wonderful things you showed me. You have a loving and romantic heart. Please don't lose that," she whispered. "We have also both grown in our faith and in Christ, and you must pass this on to our child. I want you to promise."

Valen nodded. "Okay," he whispered. "I promise."

Inside, Valen was screaming, and he wanted to know how this happened. He knew it was that truck he saw, and he wanted to find those punks and kill them with his bare hands. But he couldn't spend their last hours talking about that. He just wanted to love her.

"I love you, Rhiannon," he cried. "You made me the happiest man in the world. You're my life, and I love you. And our child will know the loving angel his mother was."

"Just love him the way you loved me, Valen. Your heart is your greatest gift, and you've made me the happiest woman in the world. You're my hero and blessed me with so much joy," she sighed.

Valen put his arms around her, and gazed into her eyes. And they kissed their last kiss.

Days past and Valen couldn't bring himself to return home. His friend Sam was kind enough to check in and feed all the animals while away.

Valen booked a room at a nearby hotel and waited for the hospital to release his newborn son from observation. He spent countless hours on the phone with police trying to track down the truck and those two kids that had stolen his whole world. But they were never found, and Valen lived and died without ever having legal justice.

When he finally mustered up the courage to return home, a deep emptiness filled his heart. Abby and the horses knew something was wrong. They simply followed him quietly as he walked the grounds. Valen entered the house slowly. It felt cold. Glasses were left out from their last dinner, and Rhiannon's shirt was thrown over the couch. He couldn't believe she was gone. It didn't seem real. Valen approached the piano and rubbed his hand across its polished wood. He tapped the keys softly, and a muffled sound echoed through the room. Upon lifting the lid to exam the problem, he found a small wrapped package with a golden bow. It was addressed to him from Rhiannon. Valen swallowed heavy, and faintness swept over his body as he opened the package. Inside was the gold wedding band she planned to give him that Christmas. As he slid it on his finger, his heart broke, and he collapsed to his knees.

Chapter XIX

For the first few years of my life, my father was a stranger to me. He often told me how much I resembled my mother. So, perhaps it killed him emotionally to even look at me. However, one day something in him changed. I remember it vividly. It was when he rushed in from visiting my mother's grave, grabbed me and told me he would never leave me alone again. My life was blessed from that day forward. I remember he used to say, "All things work together for good for those who love God and are called to His purposes. And you, my son are a blessing. My blessing."

I guess his faith and belief that all things happen for a reason and for an ultimate good helped him survive his pain. He tried to teach me to live in the moment. For at any time, our journey can end. Life is not the destination, but rather the events we experience on the road to our destination.

Although several years have passed since my mother died, and although I never knew her personally - I can feel her. I can feel her strength and energy in my veins. My father always said I had her charisma. God, I hope so. This world needs more people like her.

Dad and I grew close and when it was time for me to go to college, it was hard for me to leave him. I always felt a sense of responsibility for him and wanted to make sure that he was never alone.

I remember one night coming home from college for the weekend and searching for my father endlessly, but he was nowhere to be found. The horses in the stable had long since died and even his dog, Abby, lost all the strength in her back legs and had to be put down. My father was alone and growing old, and not knowing where he had wandered off to frightened me. In the deep recesses of my mind, I always felt fearful that depression would overtake him one day. So, naturally, when I couldn't find him, I worried.

"Dad!" I shouted out the back window. "Dad!"

"Out here," I heard a faint cry respond. "Near the tree."

I walked over to where he was. "What are you doing out here?"

"Thinking. Climb up and join me."

My dad was laid back on a giant low hanging oak limb.

"Dad - what on earth are you doing here? What if you fall?" I said as I climbed over.

"I was just gazing at the stars and thinking of all that has past and all that is to come. I've had a full life, Destin. A full life and I hope I've been a good father to you. Sometimes I think I should've, or could've done more...but I don't know. I've changed and grown so much as a person over the years, sometimes I don't recognize myself. Don't get me wrong, I've grown to be a much better person, but it's crazy to think of all the things I used to do. I've made mistakes, I know..." Valen looked straight into my eyes. "I'm rambling...Just know that I love you."

"I know, Dad. I know. Now, what's going on for you to risk falling from a tree limb and breaking something?"

"Na – I know I'm growing old and you know I'm a little crazy," he smiled. "So, I just wanted to sit here and relax. It's nice. Don't you think?" He said grinning widely. "I like remembering all the good parts of my life...marvelous," he exhaled softly.

"Dad, is anything wrong?" I continued.

"No, why are you asking?"

"I don't know, you just seem to be somewhere else, mentally."

"Well, I guess I'm just reliving the past. It was definitely an adventure! All of it - the good and the bad. I've had a blessed life, Destin. The emotions and memories amaze me. It's incredible. All the tragedies and pleasures in my life have crafted and molded me into a man I never knew I could be, and what's even more exciting is that it's not over yet. Just know I'm ready when my time comes. You don't have to worry. My faith is strong, and I'm ready to see your Mom again. I never stop missing her. Every day, I miss her and my love for her is still strong." He paused.

"I want you to remember this,' he said pointing to my chest. 'When you can love another person more than yourself, that's when you find true happiness. I had that gift with you and your mother. I consider myself very fortunate. You know, sometimes it's hard for me to distinguish the dreams from reality. Sometimes I wonder if it was all for real.'"

I put my arm around his shoulder. "It was real, Dad. I promise you. It was all real."

"Seeing you helps me realize that. You're the hopes and dreams of your mother and me brought to life. And you've always made me proud. Pursue your dreams, Destin, but don't forsake God in the process. Make the most of your life and never lose your faith, or perspective. Live with passion and know with confidence that you cannot lose when He is prioritized first and foremost. It's not about how much money, or how much prominence you have, but the impact you have on others. It's what you leave behind. How you multiply what God has given you and for His glory, not your own. I didn't know these truths early on, but thank God you do. Hallelujah - you do!" He said rejoicing with tears in his eyes.

When I think back on that night, I wish I could've said something back, but I didn't. I never said a word. Instead, my father and I just sat there for the rest of the evening enjoying each other's company and gazing at the stars.

That night is the last vivid memory I have of my father, because a week later, he died in his sleep. His friend Samuel found him, one day as he came to visit. It was a Friday evening when he discovered my Dad, curled up in a ball on the couch. The fireplace still glowed from the hot coals that burned the night before.

In his will, my Dad left me the house and what was left of the money, but most special, was his Bible, his journals and old motorcycle. I used to read the journals all the time and ride that bike all over town. I'm ashamed to say now, the bike just sits in my garage, covered with a dusty blanket and the journals are stuffed away in a box. But I keep the Bible close, as you can plainly see from what I'm holding in my hand.

We buried dad next to mom on their property, under a grand pine next to the stream they used to visit on their horses. I smile when I think of my father and mother being together again. Their souls reunited.

At that, Destin closed his Bible and stepped down from the pulpit.

Chapter XX

Hours had passed since Destin first took his position in front of the congregation at his new church. He had shared everything he knew about his beginnings and felt refocused. His congregation knew who he was now, and they all appreciated his candor and vulnerability. No one rushed out. They knew what he believed in, and why he was there. As he stood at the door greeting everyone, many passed with tear-filled eyes , and simply thanked him.

Destin looked at his watch. His wife may still be home and there was time to catch her. By sharing his past, God not only blessed others with the journey of faith shared, but He also helped Destin remember what he had forsaken. He remembered what life was truly about - Christ and learning to love as He loves, beyond self.

As Destin closed the door to the church, his body raced with energy. He could hardly keep from running. His mind seemed clearer, his body stronger, and he knew what he had to do. He was about to lose one of the greatest gifts he had been given because of his blind ambition, and he had to do something to try and save it, if it wasn't already too late.

Praying she was still there, Destin raced home and flung open the door. Lynn's nearly filled suitcase lay on the bed. Surprised, she turned around and caught his eyes with a hard, dead look. Destin could see her heart was broken, but as they stood there in the silence, the coldness in her soul began to melt. Destin took her hand and looked at the diamond wedding band still embracing her finger.

It was the same ring originally intended for his mother. Valen had given it to him the day Destin announced his engagement to Lynn. Valen knew that's where it belonged. And now, as Destin stared at it on his wife's finger, the truth behind their vows returned to him. Lynn could see the sincerity in his heart.

Without hesitation, Destin took her in his arms and held her hard against him. "I'm sorry that I have neglected you, Lynne. You are the best thing that has ever happened to me, and I can't believe what I've allowed to happen to us. I've been pursuing success, admiration and self-fulfillment through something as wonderful as ministry, but have lost sight of the big picture. My life is having you in it. It's about sharing everything together and building a strong foundation, a loving family and fulfilling our God given purpose. I have neglected my role as your husband. Please forgive me - I promise to never leave you alone, again," he cried with tears rolling down his face. "I now know what my father meant when he said those same words to me so long ago. I love you, Lynn."

Lynn stood silently weeping. She believed him, and her heart cried with joy, for she knew in her soul that he was back. The man God had given her and whom she loved was back.

Author

 Dagan is married to his college sweetheart, and they share two loving children together. They live in Augusta, Georgia where he serves as a deacon in his church, teaches adult Bible study and is active in both his community and with his family.

He enjoys teaching financial stewardship principles both at work and in his spare time, has written various books, writes for a local publication, and shares a weekly blog and devotional.

You can get and learn about many of these inspirational resources at **BendedBow.com**. While there, be sure to sign up for our free weekly devotional, and join the movement as we strive to share more hope and encouragement with others in every way – every day.

Highways End

www.ingramcontent.com/pod-product-compliance
Lightning Source LLC
Chambersburg PA
CBHW051430170626
46809CB00006B/2396